Sweetwater Ridge

By

G.L. Snodgrass

Purple Herb Publishing

Email - GL@glsnodgrass.com

http://glsnodgrass.com/

Amazon Author Page

https://www.bookbub.com/authors/g-l-snodgrass

https://www.facebook.com/G.L.Snodgrass/

Return to your favorite ebook retailer or the blog linked above to discover other works by G.L. Snodgrass. Thank you for your support.

Dedicated to

Kim Strong

Sweetwater Ridge

Chapter One

Hank Richards pulled the Big Bay into the shade of a tall ponderosa pine so he could scan his back trail. For several minutes he held still, only his eyes moving over the hills and creek area, looking for any movement, any flash of color out of the ordinary.

Eventually, he sighed as his shoulders slumped with relief. If someone was following him, they couldn't come through that cut without being seen. Some would say he was being over-cautious. But then they hadn't lived his life.

"A man after gold can't be too careful," he mumbled to his horse. The Big Bay wiggled his ears, obviously agreeing. Old Ben, the pack mule behind the horse, stomped his foot showing his displeasure at standing around and waiting.

Hank grumbled under his breath as he started back up the creek. That was the problem with living alone up in these mountains. A man started taking his animal's opinions into account.

As they climbed, he examined the country. It was laid out just like Ben Tarkington had told him years ago over that campfire out by

Pyramid Lake. Tall pines and spidery cedars. Willows down by the creek. Sagebrush and the occasional cactus. Just like any of a dozen creeks and canyons in this part of the mountains.

The man had been positive there was gold in the area, but he'd been unable to ever locate the source.

Once they'd put another two miles behind them. Hank found a spot to camp down by the creek. After staking out the horse and mule, he grabbed his pan from the pack and squatted at a likely place.

Within minutes, he had color. His heart jumped when he saw the flecks of gold at the bottom of the pan and two pickers about the size of match heads. Rough edges which meant it was close. It hadn't traveled too far.

"We'll see," he said to the approaching shadows, refusing to get his hopes up.

Too many times over the years had possibilities disappointed him. Ben wouldn't be the first man to exaggerate a little about what he had found. It sort of went with the description of a miner.

He shook his head as he made his way upstream, stopping every hundred yards to pan some more.

On the fifth pan, he came up empty. For the first time in weeks, he smiled. His face almost rebelled at the unfamiliar expression. The source had to be close. Back between this barren spot and the last pan that showed some yellow gold. But where?

Standing up, he examined the area. Steep ravine walls, rising up to a ridge behind him and sloping up and over a ridge across from him. Dry forested ground typical of the Eastern Sierra. Thick pine and cedar, sagebrush and gray fallen limbs mixed in with red jagged rocks and rough gravel.

It'd be like finding a preacher in a brothel. Near on impossible.

"It's never easy," he muttered under his breath as he started back to camp. Just once, he'd have liked to find the seam of quartz sitting out in the open instead of having to hunt and peck through the forest for it.

But then, what should he have expected? Life had never been easy. Besides, if finding the source of gold was simple. Ben or someone else would have done it years ago.

Men had been combing these hills ever since the strike in Virginia City fifteen years earlier. They'd climbed and prospected up and down these canyons yet never found anything except what they could pan from the creek.

Later that night, Hank stared up at the stars and mapped out his plans. He'd be methodical, he told himself. First, this side of the creek, only when that had been exhausted would he move to the other side.

As he lay there with his hands folded behind his head, he wondered how many nights he had spent like this. Alone, out in the far beyond. It was either this or down in some other man's mine working to get a grubstake so he could get back out here again. Someday he thought. Someday he would strike it rich.

And when he did, he'd go home, back to Cleveland, and show them what he had done.

The thought made him snort. They wouldn't remember him. He'd been nothing but a big kid living on the streets. There wasn't a person back there who would remember his name nor what he'd gone through.

The thought saddened him. It was a hard thing to realize there was no one left to impress. No one close enough to care one way or the other.

His friends Jack and Dusty would be glad for him, but they were different. They were from after he left his own version of hell.

A wolf howled in the distance, both the Bay and Old Ben shuffled at the edge of the yellow firelight. Hank sat up to toss a couple more sticks onto the fire then stared off into the night.

Prospecting was a lonely life. He well knew that. He welcomed it in fact. He'd learned long ago that the worse thing about this world was people. They had a habit of making a bad situation worse.

He'd tried over the years, but people just naturally avoided him. He'd never really figured out if it was his size that scared them off or his general cussed attitude. Either way, they left him alone and he left them alone. A situation that just seemed to work.

Probably his size, he thought with a grunt. He flashed back to a memory of the last time he'd stepped into the sutler's in Reno. A mother had instinctively pulled her small son to her side as if a grizzly bear had walked into the store.

He'd swallowed the anger inside of him and tipped his hat to her. She'd lifted her chin and turned away. He knew what she saw. A man slightly closer to seven feet than six. Beefy, with arms shaped by years of swinging a double-jack. A nasty scar over his left eye from a collapse in a silver mine. And a scowl that told people not to approach.

Now, weeks later, the look in her eyes still burned.

Turning over in his bedroll, he forced the thought away and returned to mapping out his assault on the hills around him. He'd find that source, and if he was lucky, no one could sniff at him with disdain ever again.

The next morning, after a breakfast of fresh trout, he started up towards the ridge behind him. As he wormed his way through the willows and underbrush, he used his prospecting pick to turn over stones and expose the bedrock beneath the carpet of crumbled rocks and sand.

"It could be anywhere," he cursed.

It had to be here, he thought, then reminded himself that there was just as much chance that the source had played out. A small pocket exposed to the weather. Just enough to feed the creek over thousands of years. Just enough to entice him into spending the rest of the year looking for it.

It wouldn't be the first time.

As he climbed up the ridge, his eyes constantly scanned the ground looking for any sign of mineralized quartz. That special combination of white crystals with brown, crumbly rust.

Gold could be located in other structures. But for the mother lode. The rich veins would be in the quartz.

The day grew hot and tiring as he worked back and forth, slowly climbing the ridge. He stopped for a moment and looked up at the noon sun above him. As he stood there, he pushed his hands into his lower back and tried to work out the kinks.

"It ain't going to find you," he mumbled as he started back up the hill. At this point, he'd have settled for pure quartz. At least he'd have something to test. But the ground was barren.

It was almost evening and he was heading back down to the camp with a sour attitude. It had only been the first day, but he had hoped for better results.

A large pine had fallen across the game trail, forcing him back up the hill around the exposed root ball. When he reached the top, he saw why the tree had fallen. It had sprouted in a few inches of soil over the top of bedrock.

Once it got big enough, the first strong wind had ripped it out of the ground.

He snorted at how life worked out sometimes. A good healthy tree but with no roots. It just couldn't last.

He reached out to grab a hanging root to steady himself on the slippery slope. As he did, he noticed something in the bedrock where the tree had been. A thin white streak. No more than six inches wide.

Yes, he thought. Quartz. He'd know it anywhere. Kneeling down, he brushed away more dirt, exposing a vein of quartz that extended up the side of the hill until it disappeared beneath the sand.

Hank took a deep breath and forced his heart to slow down. The stuff looked too pure. Solid white. None of the mineralization that would indicate metals mixed in with the quarts. And if there weren't no silver, iron, copper. Then, there probably wasn't any gold.

It wouldn't hurt to check, he thought as he used his pick to break away a few large chunks sandwiched between two halves of gray bedrock.

As he examined it in the dying light, a strange feeling of being watched itched between his shoulder blades. That tingly feeling that had saved his life more than once. Without any quick moves, he ducked down behind the tree's root ball. Silently cursing the stupidity of leaving his rifle in camp.

Taking a quick breath, he darted to a tall pine and slid under its overhanging branches.

No shot rang out. There was no indication that anyone was there. Just a feeling. Shaking it off and cursing himself for jumping at shadows he returned to camp. All the way scanning the country around him without being obvious about it.

That early evening, only after the canyon was bathed in shadows, he broke up the sample and panned it out. As he swished out the last of the water, he sat back on his heels. Gold. Not a lot. No more than any other pan for the day. Not enough to become rich. But enough to explore.

One thing he did know. This was the source. There was no doubt in his mind.

He froze as he glanced around. Worried that someone had seen. No one was there, he finally realized. It was five miles back to Verdi and the lumber camp and another ten to Reno. There wasn't anyone within miles, he told himself.

No, he was alone. And he had a mine to plan out.

He'd need a cabin. A sluice. Supplies. He'd need to file a claim. There were a dozen things that needed to be done.

"Don't get ahead of yourself," he mumbled as he stared down at the gold in the bottom of the pan. "Set out the stakes marking the claim. Sink a shaft and see how it turns out. That quarts might end three feet under the ground."

Stepping away from the creek, he looked into the dark towards where he'd found the vein. It might amount to nothing. But years of experience and more failures than he could count told him there was something there.

Chapter Two

Amelia Dunn refused to cry as she watched the two workmen lower her father's body into the grave. When they had finished, they both stepped back to give her time to say goodbye.

The numbness inside of her turned over to anger when she thought of the small town down the hill from the graveyard.

No one had joined her. Not one person had thought her father was worth the effort. It made her clench her teeth at the hate that burned her soul.

They'd despised him for years. And therefore, by connection, her. All because he had talked against the war. Saying they shouldn't be fighting to save slavery. That it was a rich man's war. Not his.

During the war, they had tolerated him as an ignorant farmer from the backwoods of the Arkansas Ozarks. The kind of man that could be ignored. But when the south lost. That disdain had turned to hate.

"No one likes being proven wrong," he had told her.

Amelia bit the inside of her cheek as she nodded to the workmen to fill the grave. She had said her goodbyes. Nothing was going to bring him back.

When they had finished, she reached down to pick up the carpetbag at her feet, took a deep breath, and started for the town and its train station.

Her life here was over. Some Yankee had bought the bank and called in her father's loan. The farm was gone. No, there was nothing for her here. No one to go to for help. No friends. No family.

Sighing, she pulled the slip of paper from her dress pocket and looked down at the words written on it.

Theodore Simmons, Reno Nevada.

That was all that Mrs. Davis had given her. That and a train ticket. The woman had assured her that it was common for men in the west to marry women they had never met.

The woman had been visiting throughout the county looking for brides for men out west. Surprisingly, she had been rather successful. The war had taken so many men that even now, seven years later, it was difficult to find a husband.

Amelia knew very well that she rested at the bottom of the hierarchy when it came to wife material. Plain, poor, despised locally. Not exactly big selling points. Especially for a woman at the ripe old age of Nineteen.

Most girls that had been able to find a husband had two or three children by that point.

Into this disorder, Mrs. Davis had arrived like a godsend. A way out. She had said that Mr.

Simmons was a prosperous businessman. A good man. Respected in the community. Looking for a young wife to start a family.

Amelia held her head high as she walked through town to the train station at the far end. People stopped to watch her pass. She could see it in their eyes. A combination of guilt mixed with relief knowing that she would be gone and could be forgotten. No longer a reminder of their worse tendencies.

She refused to acknowledge them as she walked. They were no longer important. They were from her past. People to be forgotten.

When it came time to board the train however, she hesitated. She was leaving everything she knew. Trusting a woman, she'd barely met. What if he didn't want to marry her? What if he changed his mind?

She scoffed. It wouldn't be worse than here. Nothing could be worse.

Taking a deep breath, she stepped up onto the train and found a seat. It would be five days. If she was frugal. She could make her funds last until she got there. If not, she would go hungry. Heaven knew it wouldn't be the first time.

She sat back as the train whistle blew. Five days. She could do anything for five days. Mrs. Davis had assured her that she would send a telegram to him informing him of her pending arrival. But Amelia didn't know if she trusted telegrams, they seemed too magical to her. A man across the nation could know she was leaving before she even left. It seemed too farfetched to even believe.

For the next five days, Amelia watched as the country changed. Several people tried to strike up conversations. But they were but passing moments. No sooner had the connection been made than it was broken when they got off the train to be replaced with new passengers.

She learned to stay to herself. It was easier that way.

When they dropped down out of the Rockies into the desert, her insides grew tighter with each passing mile. Dryer, browner, sparse. Everything was so different than at home.

"It's not home anymore," she whispered to herself as she shook her head. This would be her new home, and somehow, she would make it work.

Finally, in the late afternoon of the fifth day, the train pulled into the Reno station. Amelia ran a hand down over her best dress. A gray cotton. Poor farm girls couldn't afford silks.

She adjusted her homemade bonnet, took a deep breath, and stepped down from the train.

Two men eyed her curiously, their gaze traveling over her like she was a sow being auctioned off. She swallowed hard as she pushed away the feeling of fear that flashed through her.

"Miss Dunn?" the older of the two said with a stern expression.

She hesitated for a moment wondering if she should identify herself to these men. Something told her it might be dangerous. Neither looked like what she had imagined a prosperous businessman would look like.

They reminded her of workmen. Rough clothes, rough hands, a gun hanging on each of their hips.

"Mr. Simmons?" she asked as she held her breath.

The older one scoffed and shook his head. "He sent us," he said as he bent down to take the bag from her hand.

Amelia glanced at the younger one and shivered inside. There was something lost in his eyes. As if he didn't see the world like a normal person. A blankness that reached down to his soul.

"This is Jeb Denning," the older one said. "I'm Tom Bennet. We work for Mr. Simmons."

She noticed that neither of them tipped their hat. You would have thought that her future husband's employees might treat her with a modicum of respect.

The thought almost made her laugh. Why should things be different now? Who was she to think such a silly thought? She wasn't even married and already looking for respect and status.

"Mr. Simmons was unable to meet me?" she asked as she followed them through the train station and out onto the boardwalk.

Mr. Bennet shook his head. "Mr. Simmons is a busy man."

Amelia's stomach dropped as the reality of what was about to happen sank in. She was marrying a man who didn't really care about her. Not enough to meet her himself. It was the kind of thing that could make a woman second guess herself.

But the men who boxed her in on either side didn't give her time to ponder the situation. They urged her towards the far side of the town.

As she walked, she took in the new town. Her new home. A wide dusty street bounded by wood buildings. Most of them unpainted. Everything looked so rough. As if everything had been erected just days before.

Most of the men wore guns on their hips. There were almost no women. She swallowed hard as she once again wondered what she was getting herself into.

"Back this way," Mr. Bennet said as he indicated an alley between two buildings.

Amelia looked up at the signs above the front door. "The Red Grove?" she asked. "Mr. Simmons works in the back of a saloon?"

The young cowboy, Jeb, laughed then quickly shut it down at an angry look from Mr.

Bennet. "Mr. Simmons has a lot of different businesses. It helps to be centrally located."

She frowned as she tried to work out exactly what that meant as she followed them down the alley.

When he opened a door in the back she was hit with the stink of alcohol and the twitter of distant laughter. She had never been to a bar in her entire life. No respectable woman from home would have dared.

"In here," Mr. Bennet said as he opened a second door off a hall just inside the entrance.

Amelia held her breath as she stepped into a small bare room. A table and two wooden chairs sat in the middle. There was no window. No other door.

Her brow furrowed as she slowly turned to inspect the room. Where was Mr. Simmons? When would she meet him? Her stomach churned with worry. Everything depended on her new husband. Would he be a good man like Mrs. Davis had promised?

She turned back to ask Mr. Bennet about her future husband to find him stepping out of the room and closing the door behind him. She froze, fighting to understand. As she stood there, a heavy click echoed through the room.

Mr. Bennet had locked the door and taken the key with him.

A sense of dread flashed through her. What? Why? She rushed to the door to try the knob, but she was truly locked in this small room.

Maybe it was for her own protection, she thought. She was in the back of a saloon after all. Maybe they were worried for her safety.

Her stomach tightened into a small ball of pure worry as she fought to stop from panicking. No, Mrs. Davis had promised. Amelia took a deep calming breath. No. she would not jump to the wrong conclusions.

She removed her bonnet and placed it on the table. Mr. Bennet had put her carpetbag next to the far chair. She sat down and fought to control the rising fear inside of her. There had to be a perfectly plausible explanation and she was sure that Mr. Simmons would provide it when he arrived.

Unfortunately, he did not arrive. She was there for hours. Getting up to pace around the small room then plopping down in the chair in frustration. Really, this was unbecoming of a prospective bridegroom.

As the hours passed, she started becoming angrier and angrier. Perhaps she would not marry this man after all. If he treated her like this, what would their marriage be like?

It was then that the realization began to sink in with a thick, heavy despair. She had no money and knew no one within a thousand miles.

She thought of screaming, but what if that embarrassed Mr. Simmons? No, she would wait. She had just spent five days on a train. A few more hours wouldn't matter.

Sighing heavily, she sat back down and focused on the door, begging that it would open.

As if answering her prayer, a loud click echoed through the room as the door swung open. There in the doorway was a handsome man with blondish-red hair, tall. Dressed in tailored pants and a fancy vest over a starched white shirt with pearl buttons.

He looked at her for a moment then smiled, nodding in obvious approval. "Welcome, Miss Dunn," he said as he stepped into the room. His two employees, Bennet and Denning followed him in and closed the door behind them.

Mr. Simmons sat down across from her and continued to stare.

Amelia's insides tightened up in a mix of emotions. He was handsome. Obviously prosperous. Important traits in a husband. Yet there was something in the way he looked at her that made her cringe inside.

"I assume Mrs. Davis explained the situation and my expectations," he said.

She nodded. "Yes, she mentioned that you were looking for a young wife in hopes of starting a family."

Denning behind her snorted, causing Mr. Simmons to shoot him an angry look. He smiled at her and slowly shook his head. "It always amazes me how naive young women can be."

Her heart stopped while she frantically tried to understand.

"I believe there has been a misunderstanding," he continued. "I am not looking for a wife. Believe me, I have too many girls to ever need a wife."

"Then why did you send for me?" she asked as she fought to understand.

"To work for me, of course," he said with a smile that sent a shiver down her back.

She held her breath as the realization of her situation. "Wh ... What kind of work?"

He shrugged. "I am a brothel owner. What kind of work do you think?"

A bolt of fear flashed through her. Her worst nightmares had just come true. There had always been wild stories about this type of thing happening. But she had always dismissed it as stupid girls getting involved with things they shouldn't

The fear was replaced with a tight anger. "Mr. Simmons. I am sorry but you are mistaken. I am not that kind of woman."

He laughed. "That doesn't matter. You will be when we are done with you." He shot Bennet a quick smile. Then returned to studying her with a serious frown. "I've invested a lot of money getting you here. You will learn that I take my investments quite seriously. Now then, I'm a reasonable man. If you can repay me what I've laid out plus the money I intend to make from my investment. Then I might be willing to negotiate."

The man actually thought he was being reasonable, she realized. He was the evilest person she had ever met. A monster who thought he was justified in his action. At least the people at home had felt a touch of guilt.

Amelia's entire body buzzed with energy as she realized what she had gotten involved in. Looking around for a way to escape, she saw that both of the cowboys stood between her and the door.

"Take her to one of the cribs," he said to Bennet. "Tell Suzy she's got a new girl. She'll know what to do."

"Can I have her," Denning said with an evil sneer.

"I'm first," Bennet said, shooting his companion a hard look.

Amelia couldn't believe what was happening. These men were talking about her as if she were a piece of meat.

Mr. Simmons shrugged his shoulders. "You know the rules. I don't believe in free samples. You'll pay just like everyone else."

Denning smiled as he nodded.

Amelia felt as if she'd fallen into a different world where everything she had thought of as real was nothing but an illusion.

"Come on," Bennet said as he grabbed her arm and pulled her up out of the chair. Picking up her bag with his other hand.

"NO!" she screamed as she tried to pull away from him. These men were taking her away to rape her then turn her into a …

"Ain't much use in screaming," Denning said as he grabbed her other arm with a vice-like grip that told her she'd never get away.

"No, please," she begged Mr. Simmons as the men pulled her out of the room. The brothel owner simply watched his men drag her away without the slightest sign of emotion. To him, she was nothing but a commodity to be rented out to any man with enough money.

"You can't do this," she yelled at her two captors as they pulled her into the dark alley. "Please. You don't understand," she begged.

As the fear built up inside of her, she realized she didn't have much time. Her pleas were useless. She needed to escape immediately. Without thought, she began twisting and kicking, trying desperately to get away.

It was like trying to escape a snake's grasp. Both men held tightly, dragging her.

They ignored her fruitless attempts, being sure to stay out of range of her slashing feet. As she fought, she saw an opportunity and bit the arm holding her, sinking her teeth deep enough to draw blood. The metallic taste that filled her mouth sent a flash of hope through her.

"You crazy bi…" Bennet yelled before backhanding her across the face.

Amelia's head exploded into a thousand stars as she was knocked into the wall behind her. Her head hit the wall with a solid thud. No, she thought as a new darkness threatened to overtake her. No. if she went under they would win. No.

But the darkness grew closer. As if looking up through a narrow tube, she saw the two men looking down at her with evil smiles. Was she laying in the dirt? Both of them looked as if they enjoyed seeing her down, seeing her hurt. The look of lust in their eyes sickened her.

She was lost. Her life was over, she thought as she fought against the approaching darkness.

"Throw her over your shoulder," she heard one of them say.

Denning was reaching for her when his face turned pale as he suddenly flew away. It was as if a giant wind had picked him up and tossed him aside like a stray leaf. Bennet turned, but Amelia couldn't focus as the darkness won.

Chapter Three

Amelia pulled herself up out of the gray darkness. Wincing inside, she fought to ignore her pounding head as she tried to understand where she was without opening her eyes.

In a room, on a bed. A faint yellow light tried to peek under her eyelids.

Then it hit her as the memories rushed back into her brain. Those men. Mr. Simmons. The crib. What he wanted her to do. What they had planned for her.

Had they?

Terrified she slowly opened one eye. Too frightened to look, too frightened not to.

In the middle of the room. The biggest man she had ever seen straddled a backward-facing wooden chair. His massive arms corded with muscle resting across the backrest. Looking at her with a curious expression.

"You was out for a long time for such a small bump," he said with a shake of his head. As if he was disappointed in her.

Was he waiting for her to wake up before he raped her? Where were Bennet and Denning? Had they already …?

Without thought, she sat up and scooted to the far corner of the bed, her back against the wall. Desperate to get as far away from this man as possible.

She would fight him, she thought. But it would be useless against this giant. The man could toss her across the room without issue.

"What's your name?" he asked, unconcerned that she was quaking in the corner.

She ignored his question as she ran a hand down her dress without taking her eyes off of him. Every button was buttoned. Had they? Or had this man already taken her?

Shaking her aching head, she tried to remember. Surely, she would have known?

"This will go easier if you give me your name," he said again.

Her eyes flashed to the door. Could she get past this man? Could she escape? He was big, but he didn't look slow. He looked like solid muscle. A lot of it.

He saw her glance at the door and sat back while he brought his huge hands up. "Hey, if you want to leave, I ain't keeping you."

Amelia felt a surge of hope. Could she get free? Or would he grab her when she tried to get past? Was this some kind of sick game?

As if reading her mind, he stood up and took a step away back. She looked up and felt her jaw drop. The man was so tall and so big. It was like he took up half the room.

"You should know though," he said. "They're still looking for you."

Her brow furrowed until she realized he was talking about Mr. Simmons. Why should he care? He'd paid the brothel keeper. Obviously, they knew where she was.

"Before you leave," he continued, "do you mind telling me why I stomped them two fellows?"

She frowned as she tried to piece together what he was saying.

"You don't look like one of Simmons' girls," he added. "But hey, it takes all kinds."

"Who are you?" she asked as she tried to decipher what had happened.

"Hank Richards," he replied.

The name meant nothing to her. "What happened?"

He shrugged his massive shoulders. "I was walking past the alley. Heard a woman scream. Saw two men manhandling a woman. I sort of reacted without thinking it through and stomped 'em good. It was only then I realized they worked for Simmons. I didn't realize you were one of his girls."

"I'm not," she snapped. "And would it have made any difference? I mean if I had been one of his girls as you call it?"

Again, he shrugged. "Probably not. Like I said. I sort of reacted before my brain kicked in. I got a habit of doing that at times. My friend Dusty says it's one of my many failings."

Amelia continued to study him as she tried to work out the details of his story. The man looked angry. She wondered if it was a permanent expression, or was he mad at her for some reason? Then it hit her, she was away from her captors. Could it be true? Had this man saved her from those evil men? And if so. Did they know where she was? Would they come for her?

A sudden sick feeling filled her at the thought of them finding her. "Will they find me here?" she asked as she held her breath.

He shook his head. "Not tonight. Maybe tomorrow. If'n I know them, they'll go door to door until they find you. Simmons don't like his things being taken."

"I'm not his," she said between gritted teeth.

The huge man, this Mr. Richards, shrugged. "I bet he don't look at it that way."

"Don't they know who saved me. Won't they come straight here?"

For the first time, a hint of a smile cracked that permanent scowl. "Those two weren't conscious long enough to see who hit 'em. I'll be honest with you. It usually only takes one hit and they drop. No, they don't know. Not yet. Besides, this ain't my place. It belongs to a guy I know. Charlie is riding shotgun on a gold shipment to San Francisco. Won't be back until the weekend."

A sudden pain in the back of her head made her wince, reminding her once again of what had almost happened. She reached to the back of her head to feel a robin egg of a bump and sticky matted hair.

"Why didn't you take me to a doctor," she demanded as she looked at the small bit of blood on her fingers.

Mr. Richards snorted. "Simmons is his best customer. If it weren't for him and his women that Doctor wouldn't be able to afford his booze. I weren't sure what you wanted. Besides, it weren't that big a bump."

Amelia held out her hand with the blood on her fingers.

He shrugged. "I bleed more every Sunday after I shave. You don't need no stitches."

Her insides tightened up. The man was a callous beast. Then she thought about the coming sunup and what that would mean. Where could she turn?

"The Sheriff? I'll go to him."

Again Mr. Richards shrugged his shoulders. "You do what you want. But Simmons has him in his pocket. A lawman don't make much in these parts."

A sinking feeling of despair filled her. Every course of action seemed blocked. What was she going to do? A long cold shiver ran down her back as she tried to come up with some way out of this disaster.

She was supposed to marry, start a family. Not end up working in a brothel. Now they would be furious with her. She knew men like them. They would despise being denied, disrespected. Their pride would have been wounded and they would want to obtain revenge more than anything.

When they got their hands on her. Life would become unbearable.

Taking a big breath as her stomach turned over. What was she going to do? She looked at the man across the room and wondered about him. He'd stepped in and saved her. Why? Did he look at it as simply taking her for his own? Two bucks fighting over the females. Was that all this was?

Was it that simple? One man had her, another man had come along and taken her from him.

"Why?" she asked. "Why did you save me? What did you expect to get in return? If you thought I would become yours just because you saved me. You got another think coming. I ain't going to be yours just because you took me from some other men."

He actually laughed as he shook his head. "Don't get your hopes up. You ain't my type. I like woman smart enough not to get caught by a man like Rusty Simmons."

Her stomach clenched at his insult. No, she realized as she looked at him. He wasn't after her body. He didn't have that lustful glint in his eye. He wasn't looking at her that way. It was more the way a man looked at a horse who threw a shoe. A bother. A pain that he wished didn't happen.

"What's your name?" he asked her. "How old are you, what sixteen?"

"I'm nineteen," she told him. It had always bothered her that people thought she was younger than she was. They just naturally dismissed her too easily. Should she give him her name? It disturbed her at a gut level as if it would give him too much power. Then she almost chuckled to herself. The man was a small mountain. He didn't need more power.

"My name is Amelia. Amelia Dunn. I'm from Arkansas," she said with a heavy sigh as she tried to work out what she was going to do next.

"The way I see it," the big man said as if reading her mind, "you got two choices. Go back to Simmons. He'd probably be forgiving. You could blame it all on me. Or, hide out and hope you can catch a train to San Francisco. The next one should be along in two or three days."

A hope flashed inside of her.

"But," he continued, "San Francisco ain't no better. Probably worse for a girl all alone. There's some out there that make Rusty Simmons look like one of them tame parakeets. You wouldn't last a day on those streets. That's

32

about it unless you can come up with some other idea."

The faint hint of hope died before it had any chance. Besides she didn't have the money for a ticket.

"What then?" she snapped. "You're telling me my only choice is deciding which brothel I'm going to work in. No. I refuse."

He studied her for a long moment then nodded as he bent down and pulled a large pack up and onto his shoulders. "Well, it ain't really my problem. I shouldn't of got involved." The tone of his voice told her that he was upset at her for some reason. Or, was that just his natural way?

It was bothersome that she couldn't read him. His size and angry scowl threw everything off.

He adjusted the pack on his back, settling it on those wide shoulders. It was amazing, she didn't doubt that she would have difficulty lifting it off the ground. The man treated the pack like she treated her small purse.

She gulped when she realized he was leaving her. While she might not trust him as far as she could throw him. He had saved her. And now he was walking away. Leaving her to face her enemies all alone.

"You can't go," she said before she could stop herself.

He turned. His dark eyes boring into her. "Never did good with being told what to do. Just naturally makes me want to do the opposite."

She bit back the rising fear inside of her. "What am I supposed to do?"

He took a deep breath as if he were about to educate a dense child. "Like I said, I didn't sign on to be a nursemaid. You was in trouble. I got you out of trouble. I'd say I'd done my part. Probably more than I should have. With my luck. Simmons finds out what I did and I get barred from the Red Grove. I always liked that saloon. They got good beer. Maybe the best in town."

She looked up at him with disbelief. She was facing the worst fate possible and he was worried about getting a beer. The man was a slug. A beast. A tyrant. With the soul of a rock. He was really going to walk away and leave her to her fate.

He pulled a dark black hat off a peg and put it on. He studied her for a moment, then tipped the hat and turned to open the door. As he ducked to pass through, he turned back to her.

"Have a nice life, Amy. And there's no need to thank me." Then, he turned and disappeared into the night.

Her gut dropped as she realized she hadn't even thanked him for risking his life to save her. That thought was followed with and even worse realization. The only hope of survival had just walked out the door.

Chapter Four

Hank Richards cursed under his breath as he lifted the barrel of black powder onto Old Ben's pack. As he tied it and the bags of beans and flour to the mule's back, he shook his head.

He never should have gotten involved. See, that was what happened. He comes to town for the first time in four months and he gets wrapped up in an argument with the sneakiest scoundrel this side of Denver.

There was a gold mine he needed to protect. The last thing he wanted was a dozen of Simmons' henchman following after him. No one knew where it was. And he needed to keep it that way.

He had no sooner thought of that than he thought of a woman he had known. Sweet Kathleen. He'd have killed any man who hurt her. This woman didn't have anyone and it troubled him to think what would happen when they got their hands on the girl.

His gut turned over. He shouldn't have left her. But really, what choice did he have? She didn't want nothing to do with him. She'd made that clear enough. She'd taken one look at him and cringed like she'd seen a monster from her dreams.

Sighing, he tried to ignore what he had seen. Tried to forget that look of fear in her eyes. Then she'd flat out told him that he was the last thing she wanted in her life. As far as he was concerned, that sort of set his hands free of the entire matter.

He shook his head as he started loading the Bay with the rest of the supplies. It had taken every last bit of his dust to pay for all this. That mine had better prove out or he'd have waisted half a year of back-breaking work.

A distant rooster started to crow. He glanced up to see the sun coming up over the far horizon. His gut tightened. They'd have her within a few hours.

He shook off that sick feeling deep in his gut and shouldered his own pack. Between the horse, mule, and his own pack he'd loaded up close to seven hundred pounds of supplies. Enough to get him through the winter.

Hopefully, by next spring he'd have hit the motherload and his life would be set. If not. There were always other creeks and hillsides to explore.

But he would be thinking of her the whole time he thought as he paused and looked off into the distance. The entire time he was working, he'd be eating himself up from the inside.

"Blast it," he cursed making Old Ben shy away then look back at him like he was the worst man within a hundred miles.

"Shut up," he snapped at the mule. The animal just stood there, accusing him.

Hank took a deep breath and cursed under his breath as he grabbed Big Bay's reins and started leading him and the mule to the street and the mountains beyond. It was fifteen miles over rough broken terrain. Almost all of it uphill. It was going to a long slog, he thought.

He hadn't gone but a dozen steps when he spit into the ground and turned towards Charlie's place. Sometimes, a man just had to take action if he was going live with himself. It didn't matter if it was stupid. And this had to be one of the most idiotic ideas ever. It was just one of those traps that a man couldn't get out of. The proverbial rock and a hard place.

And he'd learned long ago, just blast his way through, and keep on going.

When he opened the door, he found her scrunched up in a corner with a frying pan in her hand. Ready to fight the devil himself.

He snorted to himself and went to the dresser on the far side.

"Here," he said as he started throwing her clothes. "Put these on. I'll never get you out of this town looking like that. Maybe disguised as a boy. Just maybe we might stand a chance."

Her brow furrowed deeply as she looked at him. The pan still raised, ready to strike. He had to admit, he did like seeing a woman willing to fight.

"Come on," he said as he indicated the pants and shirt he had thrown onto the bed. "We don't got much time. It's already too light."

She continued to frown. "Where are we going?"

"My mine. Up in the Sierras. It's the only place I can think of where you might be safe. At least until things die down and I can get you out of there."

She continued to stare at him, then the realization of what he was proposing began to sink in.

"If you think I'm going with you," she said with a snarl, "you are crazier than you look. I'm not going to be your mistress. I'm not turning one dishonor in for another."

He laughed as he bent down and retrieved an old pair of boots and tossed them to her.

"I don't need a mistress," he said as he pulled a pair of socks out of his own pack. "The only thing worse would be a wife. I ain't got the time nor the energy for such stupidity. No. you can clean and cook for room and board until I can figure out what to do with you."

She continued to frown, obviously not believing a word he said. And after the way she'd been treated by Simmons, he couldn't really blame her.

He tossed the thick woolen socks onto her lap. "Charlie's got big feet for such a small guy,"

Sweetwater Ridge

he said to her. "These will help make the boots fit."

She looked down at the socks, then the rest of the clothes before frowning back up at him.

"You're serious. You expect me to go with you to some mountain mine. All alone?"

Hank sighed heavily. She really was pretty. With nice curves in all the right places. No. He thought. Get that thought out of your head. He needed to get her out of here for one simple reason. It was the only thing that would allow him to live with himself.

Again, one of Dusty's observations. He just couldn't sleep at night unless things were as they were supposed to be.

"I'll step outside and give you a chance to change. But hurry." Without waiting for her to reply he turned and left her alone.

As he stood just outside the small shack, he watched the sun come up. Each passing second increasing the chances of them being discovered.

How long did it take a woman to get dressed? he wondered. He'd have been outfitted and on the road long ago.

This was stupid, his plan. There was no doubt in his mind. But really, it was the only way. Simmons would have the roads and trains staked out. No way were they letting this woman get away.

If people learned that a slip of a girl had pulled one over on Simmons his ruthless reputation would take a serious hit. Other people might think they could get away with things. No, a man like Rusty Simmons survived because of his reputation.

Cursing again at the loss of time, he knocked sharply on the door and barged in without a thought about her modesty. There were more important issues at play.

He found her with her back to him as she tucked Charlie's red flannel shirt into his pants. Hank's gut fell. There was no way anyone would ever think she was a girl. Not if they saw her from behind. Then she turned to him, her eyebrow raised in question.

Nope. Not from the front either. The woman was just too female. Too many curves and a soft angelic face. She looked as much like a boy as Old Ben looked like a badger.

"What do you think?" she asked.

He scoffed and shook his head. "It will never work. You're too much woman."

Her face fell in disappointment but not before a brief look of satisfaction.

He studied the situation for a moment. Jack or Dusty would know what to do. But they were way out of town and no way was he bringing Simmons men down on them and their families. No, he needed to solve this one himself.

Then it hit him. He gave her a quick smile as he pulled off his coat and tossed it to her. Then removed his hat and placed it on her head. It slipped down almost to the bridge of her nose. She looked like a little kid in her dad's clothes.

She frowned obviously not believing it would work then slipped into the thick canvas jacket. The coat hung halfway to her knees and the sleeves fell to below her fingers.

"Here," he said as he rolled the sleeve up to her wrists. "We'll give you some gloves to hide those hands. Keep the hat low. And maybe they won't recognize you."

"Do you really think this will fool them."

"Don't know," he answered. "But it hides the curves."

She continued to frown as he went to the stove and wiped soot onto his fingers. "This might help," he said as he smoothed the soot along her chin line. As he did, he paused for a moment when he realized just how soft and tender her skin was.

It was enough to make a man rethink everything he thought he knew about the world.

She pushed the hat back to look up into his eyes. The two of them stood there looking into each other's eyes until she broke the gaze and said, "I'll finish it."

He nodded as he grabbed her carpetbag and took it outside to add to Old Ben's pack. He stuffed it up under the canvas cover. Making sure that nothing was exposed.

This was such a big mistake. The last thing he needed was a guest. She'd get in the way. Pestering him for things that took him away from his work. No, this wouldn't work. He wasn't set up for a woman.

The thought made his stomach clench up tighter than a preacher's purse. He could see it in her eyes. She didn't trust him and never would. Only the threat of death and dishonor were worse than going with him. Even then it was almost a toss-up in her mind.

Was she trading one monster for another?

He'd just finished adjusting the packs when he heard a sound behind him. He turned to see a slight figure swamped in an old coat, head down, the hat brim hiding her face. But he couldn't get the view of her dressed in Charlie's pants out of his head.

"Do you think it will work?" she asked when she looked up. "I put a piece of cloth in the hatband to make it fit."

He sighed heavily. "We'll see. We don't really got much of a choice."

She took a deep breath. He could see the hesitation in her eyes. She so didn't want to do this. But finally, she nodded and closed the door before walking up to him.

"This is Bay," he said indicating the big horse. "And that's Old Ben. Be careful. He's like me. He bites and kicks."

She smiled as she turned to the mule and held out her hand. Hank's jaw dropped when the normally cantankerous beast nuzzled her hand then gently butted her with his head. It was impossible. Two seconds and she'd become the mule's best friend.

"He's sweet," she said as she glanced back over her shoulder at him with a frown as if he'd lied to her.

Hank shook his head. He'd seen that mule chase after dogs with a hateful gleam to his eyes. He'd been known to kick out stalls and had a habit of taking a chunk out of anyone who wasn't paying attention.

Now he was looking at her like a lost puppy.

He rolled his eyes. "Great, you take him, I'll take Bay. If someone says anything. You let me do the talking."

She swallowed hard then nodded.

The two of them lead the animals out onto the street then turned west. Hank scanned the buildings on either side looking for any sign of danger. A cowboy with too much curiosity. A shopkeeper who couldn't mind his own business.

From the corner of his eye, he kept an eye on Amy. "Stop walking like a girl," he cursed at her.

"Shut up," she grumbled from under her hat without looking up.

He almost laughed but then he saw two men approaching down the boardwalk towards them. His gut tightened. They weren't weaving and joshing like two men returning after a night of carousing. No, they had to be Simmons' men.

Without being obvious, he made sure his gun rested free in his holster as he slowly guided The girl and the mule to the far side of the road.

They were almost past when one of the cowboys stopped. "You and your boy are off early, Richards."

Hank's guts shifted to full battle mode as he let his hand drop just a little closer to his gun. If they discovered the truth, he'd pull the gun and use it to get them out of there.

Of course, he could take out two or three. But Simmons had a dozen men. They'd get him eventually. Especially if it went to guns.

"Us miners don't got the easy life you boys do," he said to them.

The other cowboy laughed and shook his head. "You're supposed to ride horses. Not lead them."

Hank shot him a quick glare. The cowboy swallowed quickly. He'd made a mistake. Teasing a man like Hank. He knew his reputations. There was more than one man in this town who had paid for crossing a line.

The cowboy decided it was better that they move on. He grabbed his friend and pulled him to continue their search.

Hank sighed internally and glanced over at Amy. His heart lurched. The girl was shaking like a leaf in a strong wind.

"Steady," he whispered to her. "They're gone."

"I thought for sure they would discover me," she whispered back.

Hank snorted. "Men only see what they expect to see. Especially when it comes to women. They get ideas in their head and they can't shake them. Sort of comes with being a man. Ain't right, but it's real.

Chapter Five

It wasn't until they got out of town before Amelia could take a full breath. She had been terrified.

The worst had been those two cowboys. She had seen how Hank's hand had hovered over his gun. He'd been ready to kill or be killed. All because of her. Who was this man? She knew nothing about him. Yet, here she was, walking into the mountains with him.

The thought sent a shiver down her spine. Had she jumped from the pan to the fire?

Ever since he'd barged back into the shack and started throwing clothes at her, she had been struggling to understand. At first, she'd been ecstatic that he had come back for her. Only to have that ray of hope shattered when he talked about taking her to his mine. Taking her up into the mountains all alone.

But really, what choice did she have? She'd known as soon as he left the first time that he was her only hope and her prayers had been answered. But everything about him yelled a warning. His sheer size. That permanent scowl. The way he talked to her as if she were a burden to be tolerated.

The man was a beast at heart. Her only hope was that he was the kind of beast that would not force a woman against her will.

Then there had been the whole issue of wearing men's clothes. She'd felt exposed, standing before him in pants. Then she'd seen it in his eyes. Admiration. The kind of look that made a woman feel good about herself.

Then, just as fast, it was gone. Replaced by his normal scowl as he complained about how much she didn't look like a boy.

Deep inside she'd been torn. Upset at failing. Then worried that if he saw her as a woman, he would come to expect something from her. Something she was unwilling to give.

What did he expect from her? she wondered. And how could she ever stop him from taking what he wanted? The man was so large and as solid as a rock. Once they were out there, she would be even more vulnerable.

Sighing heavily, she pushed back the fear and worry and focused on walking like a boy but the constant upward grind was taking its toll on her. The heavy boots and the growing morning heat were making her feel like a wrung-out dishtowel.

They had walked about an hour and she was almost going to surrender and ask him to stop for a moment when he led them to the shade of a large cottonwood tree by the side of the road.

"Got to adjust the packs," he mumbled. "Things settle after a bit."

She nodded as she took deep breaths and tried to regain her strength. She pulled at the pants. Her legs were going to be raw by the end of the day walking in these rough clothes. And the boots weren't any better. Her feet swam in them. Even two pair of socks didn't take up the space.

She looked down at his boots and almost laughed. If she was having problems with this Charlie's, she'd have been lost inside of Hank's.

"Come on," he snapped as he started again. "We got a long day in front of us."

"Do you really think we got away?"

He paused for a moment then nodded. "For now. It might take them a while. But eventually, they'll put it all together."

"Will they come after us?" she asked.

He shrugged. "Maybe. I had to file a mining claim at the Assay Office. Once they figure out it was me. They'll know where we're at. That clerk would sell his mother to keep in Simmons' good graces."

Her insides quivered with the thought of being discovered. "How would they know it was you?"

"Don't know. But things just have a way of going bad."

She swallowed hard as she contemplated being discovered and taken.

"Hopefully," he continued when he saw the fear in her eyes, "you'll be long gone before they get there."

She frowned. "But what about you? You will be all alone."

He scoffed. "I been alone my whole life. They come after me, they'll learn they've bitten off too much."

His confidence didn't seem like bravado to her. He was just speaking the facts as he saw them. If someone attacked him and his mine. It would be like going into a den after a bear. He'd tear them apart then return to mining.

The thing was, deep down, she believed him.

Without another word, he started up the road. Amelia hurried to catch up. They continued walking between the railroad tracks and the river.

As they climbed, she kept looking over at him expecting him to talk. She had a thousand questions she wanted to ask. But the man was tighter than Kentucky twins. Finally, she couldn't resist.

"Where are we? And how far is it?" she asked as she fought to catch her breath.

He sighed heavily as he continued to walk forward, bent slightly under the weight of his heavy pack.

"That's the Truckee River," he said pointing to the side. "Those are the rails that lead up over the Sierras to San Francisco."

She nodded as she looked up at the towering snow-capped mountains in front of her.

"This is the path that Donner party took back in the forties," he said glancing at her to find out if she'd heard the story.

She grimaced when she thought about people who had resulted to cannibalism to survive.

"Up a way is Verdi, mostly a logging camp supplying the mines with timber."

Nodding, she glanced over at him, silently urging him to tell her more.

He sighed heavily. "After Verdi, we'll branch off up my creek to the mine."

And that was it, she realized. All the information he was going to give her. As if that answered everything she needed to know.

Sighing heavily, she focused on keeping up. The man set a fast pace. His long legs eating up the distance. It took everything she had not to be left behind. Something told her the man wouldn't be upset if she fell out.

In fact, he'd probably prefer is she just gave up and went back to Simmons. It would make his life so much easier for him. He wouldn't have to waste time taking care of her and wouldn't have to worry about men tracking him down.

She set her jaw and bent forward to continue climbing. She refused to give him an excuse to abandon her. Not out here.

The country around her was so open. So vast. Different than the hills of home. Back there, the land was covered in trees and underbrush. And you couldn't go a mile without running into another person.

Here, they'd traveled six miles or so and hadn't seen another person. The sparsity was amazing. And when she looked forward, she shuddered at the snowcapped mountains in front of them. So high. It made her quiver inside at the thought of having to cross over them.

Breathing hard, she fought to keep up.

"Got to check the horse's hooves," he snapped suddenly as he pulled to a stop.

Amelia sent up a silent prayer as she fought to regain her breath. He spent several minutes using his knife to clean the bottom of their hooves then adjusting the packs. Just long enough for her to regain her strength. Then they were off again.

And he's doing it with a hundred-pound pack, she thought. The man was like a bull. Indestructible. And just as talkative.

They'd spent half the day together and he hadn't said a dozen words since leaving town. She bit back a nasty comment. There was no reason to upset him. Besides, it would have taken too much energy to get into a fight with him over his lack of social skills.

As they climbed, the landscape changed. The sagebrush shifted over to tall pine trees and the occasional cedar. Again, different than home. Bare patches of ground between each tree. At home, the area would have been covered in underbrush.

"Keep your head down," he whispered sharply.

Of course, she looked up to see what was bothering him. Angry at the thought of being told what to do. Then she immediately dropped her head when she saw what was in front of her.

They'd come around a bend in the trail to find a logging camp in the distance. Men were using a sawmill to form large timbers. She immediately ducked her head as her heart raced. Would anyone recognize her? Had Simmons sent men here to wait for them?

These and a dozen other fears flashed through her. If Simmons got his hands on her he'd never let her escape. He'd use her for years then toss her away when she was no longer of value. Her life would be ruined.

"Hey, Hank," a man yelled as they walked by the group of men.

Hank nodded back but continued walking, making sure he and both horses were between her and the men.

"Hold up," the man said as he began walking towards them.

Hank grumbled under his breath but he stopped to wait for the man. Amelia's heart raced as she studied the ground in front of her. Torn between keeping her head down and looking up to see what threat was approaching. All while trying to suck in enough air to fill her empty lungs.

"You find anything up there," the man said pointing up into the mountains.

Hank scoffed and shook his head at the packs on the horses. "You're looking at a year's worth of work. Could of made more punching cows."

The man smiled. "Or cutting trees. You want, we'll take you back. Never knew a man could swing an ax like you. Heck, we're so short-handed, we'll even take on the boy."

Amelia held her breath. Please, she begged, get rid of him before he discovered the truth.

Hank snorted. "He ain't good for much. It'll be years before he puts on enough muscle to do a man's work. Only took him on to have someone to talk to."

The man laughed. "Yeah right. Now I know you're finding color. An ornery cuss like you ain't never needed someone to talk to. Or is it that you're needing help in your old age?"

Amelia held her breath. What if Hank reacted to the insult? She could well imagine him getting into a fight and the truth about her being exposed. Instead, he surprised her by giving out a short laugh.

"Preston, the day I need help working a mine is the day I walk away and take on women's work. Like maybe cutting down trees."

The man laughed and slapped Hank on the shoulder. "You change your mind. We got a place for you."

"I'll remember it," Hank said as he pulled at Bay's lead while shooting her a quick glance to keep up and keep the horses between her and the men.

As they walked away, she could feel the man's eyes on her. She was positive if she turned, she'd see a curious frown. Either that or worse, a knowing look as if he had discovered a secret.

She held her breath for a dozen yards. Until they were far enough away she could let it out with a loud whoosh.

Hank laughed and shook his head. She would have been relieved until she realized he was laughing at her, not with her. Her blood ran cold. The man was a monster. They'd been within inches of being discovered. Of course, she had been terrified. And he laughed at her.

"You're mean," she snapped without looking at him.

He chuckled again. "Preston is blinder than a dead bat. I could have had one of them English princesses leading my mule and he wouldn't have seen her."

She bit her tongue as she fought to hold off with an angry response. But after another twenty yards, she couldn't hold it back any longer.

"Not only that, but talking disparagingly about women's work is not very nice. I can assure you that you have no idea how hard women work."

He snorted as he growled under his breath. "Ain't nothing about women," he said as he spat into the dirt. "I ain't ignorant. Even if I don't know what disparaging means. I can figure it out. And I know some women work hard. I done seen it."

She blanched as she realized she had made him angry. Truly upset. But still, she couldn't stop herself. He'd made her upset as well.

"Then why refer to women that way?"

He grumbled and shook his head as if he thought she was dumber than the mule she was leading. "Because," he said, "I needed to cut him down as quick as possible so he'd leave us alone and those were the words that would do it without making him want to fight."

"I still think ..." she began.

"Stop thinking," he cursed. "It will just get us both in trouble. You leave this stuff to me. I'll get you away from Simmons. Either that or you're more than welcome to go off on your own. Let me know and I'll get down your bag."

Her stomach fell when she realized he was serious. He was perfectly willing to let her go. Let her walk away. The realization shifted something inside of her as she bit the inside of her cheek.

Just shut up Amelia, she told herself. She needed this man. At least until she could come up with something better. This was a hard, harsh land.

"Also, just so you know," he continued, "every one of those men back there are frequent customers of Rusty Simmons and his girls. And yes, most of them would have treated you fair. They'd have been more than willing to give you a ride back to town.

"But," he continued, "there are more than one or two on that crew that I wouldn't trust with my horse. Let alone a pretty woman. They'd take you halfway to town then off into the bushes. So, you keep that in mind if'n you want to take off."

She shuddered as she hurried to keep up with him. Was it always going to be like this? Every way she turned was filled with danger. Home was stacked with people who hated her. Reno held a monster named Simmons. The lumberjacks couldn't be trusted.

And next to her was a large man who hated her and the trouble she brought on him.

Fighting back a tear, she ground her teeth. She would find a way to get away. She had to.

Chapter Six

Hank pulled up so that he could look back down the trail. He'd been doing this all day. Finding excuses to give her a rest. He'd have been home hours ago, but he couldn't push hard like he wanted to. The woman wouldn't have been able to hold up.

Sighing, he shook his head.

"Stay on the bedrock," he told her when he was satisfied they weren't being followed.

She frowned at him.

He pointed to the long stretch of solid rock to the side of the creek. This was his secret. The path next to the rail line was heavily traveled. At least for this part of the country. Their tracks would be lost in amongst a dozen others from the last month. They'd never discover that he'd left the trail. By stepping off onto solid rock, no one would notice fewer horseshoes or boots on the main trail if they didn't see any leaving it.

"You go first," he said pointing off the trail and up the creek. "And stay on the hard rock. It don't leave no tracks."

Awareness finally crossed her face, as she smiled and started up the hard outcropping. He watched as she climbed. She'd removed his heavy coast once they had passed the lumber camp and hung it over Old Ben's pack. Now, he could only admire the view as her hips swung side to side in a figure-eight motion that could put a man in a trance.

When she moved like that, there weren't a man in the world who would think she was a boy.

Shaking it off, he grumbled under his breath. He was going to have to find a way to get her out of there. Hips like that could make a man forget about his work.

Once they were through the cut and well into the ravine, he stopped again and watched the cut. If they were being followed, their pursuers needed to hurry before it got too dark and they lost the trail.

His insides tightened up at the thought of Simmons and his men coming after this girl. It was ridiculous but he felt a protectiveness for her. He'd barely known her for a day, and yet, his gut rebelled at the thought of anything bad happening to her.

"Come on," he snapped as he moved past her to lead the way up the trail towards his mine. He caught her giving him a quick frown, obviously wondering what she had done to upset him.

It wasn't her. Well, not totally. It was more about the situation. A woman was going to make his life a complete mess. He just knew it. No, he needed to figure out a way out of this disaster. He should just take her to Sacramento. Maybe he could find some preacher and his wife who would take her in.

Of course, those were far and few between.

Swallowing his anger, he continued up the thin trail next to the creek. As he walked, his shoulders began to twitch with that familiar feeling of being watched. He'd been having it on and off ever since he'd walked up this canyon earlier that year.

It wasn't Simmons' men. They couldn't have gotten ahead of him. No, it was something else but he'd never been able to place it but he knew it was true. He'd learned when he'd lived on the streets. A boy didn't last long unless he could sense danger before seeing it.

Then there was the Army. Those four years of war had honed his senses to a fine point. He usually knew the enemy was there before he saw him. And he could see a thousand yards through the trees. It was one of the many things that had kept him alive. That and being the meanest, toughest idiot in the area.

"What do you think, Amy?" he asked as he stopped to give the horses a drink and her a break.

"It's beautiful," she said with surprise as she pressed her hands into her lower back while looking up and down the creek.

He nodded. "Yeah, it do grow on you. I like to hear the creek gurgling at night. The birds wake me in the morning, and the days don't get too warm down here. There's a deep pool by the cabin that's bluer than Sonoran Desert Turquoise."

She was silent for a moment then frowned at him. "Why do you call me Amy? My name is Amelia? And do you expect me to call you Hank? It seems rather informal."

He shrugged his shoulders. "Just seemed right. Calling you Amy. You look like an Amy. Innocent, sweet, pure trouble. Does it bother you?"

She bit her lip as she shook her head. "My grandpa used to call me Amy."

"As for calling me Hank," he continued, "you can call me anything you want but Henry."

Her brow furrowed. "Why not Henry? That is your given name isn't it."

His stomach clenched up. He hated talking about this stuff. It was better forgotten but he could see she wouldn't stop until he gave her an answer. See, this was what happened when a man took on a partner or helped a damsel in distress. They had a habit of asking questions he didn't want to answer.

"That was my father's name," he said through gritted teeth. "And I don't like being reminded of the connection."

She continued to frown. "You didn't get along with your father?"

He scoffed. "Let's just say. I took a beating every day until I was big enough to fight back. When I got done with him, he couldn't raise either arm to hit anyone ever again."

Amy winced as her eyes narrowed in sadness and concern. "How old were you?"

He took a deep breath and shook his head. "Twelve. He weren't a big man. I think he believed my ma strayed. That was the only thing that explained my size and was what probably made him meaner than a trapped snake."

The look in her eyes had been like a sharp knife to the gut. A combination of pity and fear. It had been as plain as day all across her face. That doubtful fear where she wondered just how much of a monster he was.

"Let's go," he snapped to Big Bay to start up the trail. He didn't look back but listened to make sure she followed. When he heard a twig snap and Old Ben blow with a heavy snuff. He knew she was following.

His heart pounded in his chest. It always did when he thought about those years. He gritted his teeth and shook his head as he tried to push down the anger rising inside of him.

See, he thought. He could have gone all day without that feeling of failure if he'd been alone. But no, he was partnered up with a nosy female. And deep in his heart. He knew she wouldn't let it rest. Somewhere along the way she'd bring it up again and poke at him with more questions.

That was the difference between men and women. He'd been friends with Jack and Dusty for years and they'd never pried into his past.

One day with this woman, and she wanted to know every secret.

Grumbling to himself, he tried to focus on getting home to his mine. Getting back to where he belonged. Back to doing what he was supposed to do. Maybe if he could start swinging a double-jack he could get rid of this feeling of pending doom.

.oOo.

Amelia watched his massive shoulders and narrow hips as he walked up the trail in front of her. Not for the first time she wondered about him. He was so rough. So prickly when it came to his past. Would she ever learn who he truly was?

Doubtful, she realized with a sick feeling. Her very life might depend upon this man and she knew nothing about him.

He was big, cantankerous, and he'd saved her when he didn't have to. He liked being alone. It was obvious. The further they got away from people the more he seemed to relax. At least a little. Which for him was probably a lot.

What else did she know? Nothing. And she was all alone with him. What kind of fool did that make her?

A feeling of trapped helplessness filled her for the thousandth time that day. What choice did she have?

None. She could do nothing but follow this man up this trail and pray it all worked out.

The sun had crossed the western ridge and cast the canyon in shadows when they came around a sharp bend in the creek. There was the deep blue pool of water he mentioned. He pulled up and looked back at her. Amelia stopped to examine the area.

A small log cabin sat on a bench a dozen feet above the creek. The building couldn't have been more than fifteen feet square with interlocking pine logs and a sod roof over log polls. A rough stone chimney peaked above the gable at the far end. A door on one side and a shuttered window on the other.

Several tools hung on the side of the cabin walls. A long crosscut saw, a big double headed ax, even a scythe.

Her stomach fell. It was even smaller than her father's shack back in Arkansas. And this man next to her would make it feel even smaller.

She swallowed as she tried to talk herself into believing that it wouldn't matter. All the while wondering what would happen that night when it was just the two of them alone in that small space.

Taking a deep breath to steady her racing heart, she spun to inspect the rest of the property.

Down by the creek was a long trough up on stilts. She frowned at him and indicated the structure.

"Sluice flume," he said with the first real smile she'd ever seen on him. "Takes water from up the creek, load it with crushed ore from the shaft. It washes everything away and leaves the gold. At least if I'm doing it right."

She nodded as she began to see how it would work.

"Don't use it for drinking water," he told her as he slipped out from his heavy pack and rolled his shoulders. "I got it set at just the right level. Besides, If I'm washing oar, it gets a bit milky with clay and stuff."

Again, she nodded. "Where is the mine?" she asked as she looked around.

"The shaft is up there," he said as he pointed to a point up in the trees. "Follow the corner of the outhouse and you can see it." A gash of crumpled gray rock helped her find it. The tailings from inside the mine, she realized.

"Come on," he said as he opened the door and stepped back.

Amelia held her breath as she stepped into the darkness. A simple table, two chairs. A wooden floor. A flat hearth in front of the chimney with a swinging metal arm to hold pots over the fire. Shelves along the wall that held a few pots and pans, neatly folded clothes, empty flour sacks, and several cured deer hides.

At the far end of the top shelf, a small jar and small tin box stood out. A finely crafted wooden chest was centered on the floor underneath the shelves.

Everything in its place, she realized. The man was organized. She had to give him that.

And there, at the far end of the cabin, a very long single bed attached to the wall. She gulped as she quickly looked away so that he wouldn't read her thoughts.

"I'll sleep up in the mine shaft," he said.

Her heart jumped. He'd known instantly what she feared most and reassured her.

"Never did like sleeping around other people," he mumbled under his breath as he went back out to start unloading the packs. "Can't rightly settle."

She could only stand there and shake her head. Never assume he was being kind, she thought to herself. He was sleeping in the mine for himself, not her. Never give him the credit. The man was a cantankerous beast and she should never forget it.

Chapter Seven

For the next hour, they unloaded the supplies. The girl could only stand there and watch him lower the bags of flour and beans into a root cellar behind the cabin. He'd built a stronghold buried in the bank of the mountain and lined it with thick logs.

He'd been right, he thought with confidence. She didn't look like an Amelia, more like an Amy.

Her brow continued to furrow as she tried to understand her new surroundings.

"Keeps out the bears," he said as he dropped the heavy lid before locking it in place. "And don't be going in there in the dark with a lantern or candle."

Her brow furrowed in question.

He sighed heavily. "I keep the coal oil and black powder down there. You set that off and it'd take out half the mountain. They'd never find enough of us to fill a thimble."

She gulped when she realized it would be but a few feet from where she slept each night.

After things were put away. He lit a lantern, placed it in the middle of the small table and started making a quick meal of pemmican and hardtack.

Her stomach rumbled, she hadn't eaten anything but some berries on the trail and a piece of pemmican all day.

As the two of them sat at the table and ate in silence. She tried to gather in all the facts she would need to know. He'd shown her his small pot of sourdough. Where he kept the salt and pepper.

"So, cooking and cleaning?" she said as she used her fingers to break the hardtack. "All we have is flour and beans and enough pemmican for a small army."

He snorted. "There's a slab of salt pork hanging in the larder. We got berries in the hills. Fish in the creek. Blue grouse in the grass and the occasional deer makes its way through. I'll see if I can get one the next day or so. We've also got wild onions and a dozen different greens. And if we get desperate. There are always pine nuts. We ain't going to starve."

Amelia nodded as she looked around the small cabin. Her gaze came to rest on the double-barreled sawed-off shotgun hanging on pegs above the door. He'd placed his rifle on the pegs above it and hung his gun belt on a hook beside the door.

"Can you shoot?" he asked when he saw where she was looking.

She laughed. "I was barking squirrels before I could read my letters. My father never had a son. So he sort of just taught me instead.

Hank nodded in appreciation. "Well, that shotgun is loaded. It's good against bears or wolves. It kicks worse than Old Ben. If Simmons' men show up. You grab that gut buster and come find me. A man ain't going to argue with that weapon. You can't miss and it's likely to tear a hole in him so wide you could drive a steer through him."

She swallowed as she nodded. The thought of killing a man tore at her stomach but deep down she knew she could do it. If it was the only way she could remain free, she'd do it.

For the first time that day she felt safe. Here in this cabin in the wilderness. No one knew she was there. Yet a feeling of hope began to fill her.

"How long do you think we will have to hide here?" she asked. "Before I can get away."

He scoffed and shook his head. "Like I said, you can leave whenever you want. I ain't holding you."

Her heart jumped. He was upset for some reason. She hadn't been criticizing him or his home. Why did he take everything as an insult? It was like walking on eggshells around this man.

Taking a deep breath, she let it out slowly to control her anger. "I was just curious. I am very appreciative for what you have done for me. There is no reason to be mad at me. I was just asking a question."

Grunting, he took another bite of pemmican. "Yeah, well, don't mind me. I got a habit of biting first without thinking things through. One of my many failings my friend Dusty says."

"You have friends?" she asked sarcastically then froze, terrified she'd overstepped some hidden boundary.

He stared hard at her, then threw his head back and laughed. A hard, belly laugh. For the first time, she saw a different side of him. A man with more than one dimension. Something more than just beast.

"You got sand. I'll give you that," he said as he continued to chuckle. The mood inside the cabin changed a little, she realized. It was as if some new arrangement had been reached. Almost like he preferred it when she pushed back.

That was it, she realized. He didn't like victims. He preferred a person who could hold their own. The realization opened a new world to her. She didn't have to be careful around him. His bark was way worse than his bite.

"Ain't no station between Reno and Sacramento," he said as he shook his head. "Once them locomotives start up the mountains they don't like stopping. And ain't no need for coal or water."

She nodded as a sinking feeling began to fill her.

"I can't take you to Jack's or Dusty's. Their wives would take you in. But I don't want them

70

on the wrong side of Simmons. They got families they need to worry about."

Again, she nodded. It was the right thing, she realized though she would have loved to talk to his friends and their wives. If only to learn more about the man.

"So ..." he said with a heavy sigh. "We'll give it a couple of weeks, maybe a month then I'll take you over to Sacramento. Use the horses. Old Ben likes you. He might let you ride him. Maybe we could find you a nice family to stay with in Sacramento."

She sighed. A month. The thought made her shudder.

"Any earlier," he continued, "and they might be waiting for us in Truckee. We can't get up over those mountains without going through Truckee. Any later and the snows will close the pass to horseback."

She gulped as she thought about the Donner Party being caught in those snows.

"A month," she said with a hesitation. "I will try to not get in your way."

He laughed. "That ain't likely. But you go ahead and try."

Amelia swallowed a nasty comeback. The man was rude and unfeeling, she told herself. There was no reason that she had to fall to his level. Instead, she lifted her chin and ignored him.

Of course, it had absolutely no impact. The man was denser than the rock he mined. As far as he was concerned, the less she talked the better.

Swallowing a deep sigh, she looked over at the bed then at her carpetbag. She stood up and started pacing. The small cabin felt like it was squeezing at her. As she turned, she caught him looking at her hips.

A sudden burst of shame washed through her. She was prancing around in men's clothes. Of course, he was going to look at her that way.

She quickly sat down again, being sure to grab her bag and hold it on her lap.

He took a moment to finish his meal. She knew that he was perfectly aware she wanted him to leave her so she could change into proper clothes. But the man refused her any kindness until he was done.

Eventually, he stood up. His size making the cabin shrink.

"See you in the morning," he said as he grabbed his rifle with one hand, a wool blanket, and the lamp with the other. He was halfway out the door when he frowned, shook his head, and came back in to light the second lamp before turning and leaving again.

Amelia could only sit there with her mouth open. The man had the social understanding of a tree stump. Nothing about how she would be safe in a strange cabin in the far woods. Nothing about having a good night.

She'd known men to treat their dog better than he treated her. It was enough to make her anger bubble just below the surface. If it wasn't for the danger she faced, she would leave and never have to deal with him again.

How would she be able to put up with it for a month? And then what? A long heavy trip over the mountains to some unknown future. Her stomach turned over. Would she ever know peace again? Would she ever feel truly safe?

The thought filled her with a longing for her father's home. She missed him so much. He had been the one true thing she knew in this world. An honorable man who had worked himself to death. A man of principle.

But he'd also been the most unlucky man she had ever known. Or at least that was what it had seemed at the time. The Confederate Army took what little he could grow and paid with worthless paper. Crops that failed. Sick stock. A thieving banker. Every step along the way. He had failed. Barely able to keep their heads above water.

And now, here she was in the western mountains with a small giant. Running from an evil fate.

No, she thought as she set her shoulders. She would not succumb to the depression that threatened to overtake her. No, she would not become a burden to Hank Richards. At least she could control that much about herself.

Later that night, with the lamp turned down, she lay in the darkness and thought about the man asleep up in his mine shaft. At no time had he made demands of her. Why? Was there something wrong with her?

It had been her experience that males thought of little else. Whether they were dogs, bulls, or human. They all had one thing on their minds. Was Hank the one honorable man? She had seen the way he had looked at her. He liked what he saw. Appreciated it at a very male level and it had lit the female part deep inside of her.

It made her very aware of him as a man. After all, he had all the manly attributes. Size, muscles, a square jaw, and sharp eyes. And when he wasn't scowling he was almost handsome. Even the scar above his eye made him look dangerous.

No, there was definitely a man woman thing between them. Yet he had made no move to take what he wanted.

She rolled over on the thin feather mattress and punched at the pillow. Could she count on him keeping his hands to himself? The troubling thought gnawed at her until she finally fell into a deep sleep.

The next morning, she woke to the chirping of birds and the gurgle of the creek. She smiled herself. He was right, it was a pleasant way to wake in the morning.

The faint light showing from beneath the shutter let her know that he would be there soon. For some reason, she believed he was not the type of man to waste the day. She jumped from the bed and rushed to get dressed before he appeared. The last thing she wanted was him coming in and finding her in her night shift.

Once she had donned her dress, she took a deep calming breath. It felt so wonderful to wear women's clothes again. It gave her a sense of being armored against the world. As if it provided protection.

A distant curse let her know he was coming. She opened the door to see him walking down the trail pushing at his lower back and rolling his shoulders as if he were trying to work out the kinks.

"Good morning," she said. "If you had chickens I would make you eggs for breakfast."

"This is a mine, not a farm," he grunted as he grabbed the saw off the wall and stomped to the woodpile. "If I wanted a farm I'd of lived on the flatland."

She shook her head. "Well, good morning to you, too."

He grunted again then began to saw wooden planks from a long log. His wide shoulders and strong arms making quick work of it. When he was done, he gathered them up and came back towards the cabin.

"What are you doing?" she asked him with a furrowed brow.

"Making a bunk," he said. "I ain't sleeping on the ground again. Not when I got a perfectly good cabin. Don't make sense."

Her heart fell. He'd had a miserable night. All because of her. Then the realization that they would be sharing the cabin at night hit her with a sharp wallop.

She swallowed hard as she went back inside and started a fire to make biscuits from the dough she'd started the night before. At least she could do that for him.

He worked in the corner, building a bed above the existing bunk. She would be sleeping directly above him, she realized. Obviously, she thought with a laugh. No way was he sleeping in the top bunk. If it collapsed she'd be crushed.

As she slid the biscuits out of the pan onto a pewter plate, she grumbled inside. It seemed wrong to serve them without butter. Or at least a heavy gravy.

"Come eat something," she said. "We can't have you wasting away."

He snorted an almost laugh then set down his hammer to come to the table.

"At least it's better than hardtack," she said as she watched him eat.

He grunted, but he nodded and took a second, then a third. Well, at least he appeared to like them. Not enough to comment. But he hadn't turned his nose up at them.

Once he was done, he returned to working in the corner then turned to her. "If you need something to do. You could stake out the horses down by the creek where they can get some good grass."

She swallowed. The man was one of those that couldn't stand to see someone standing around not doing anything. Very well, she thought as she left to tend the horses. It was going to be like that. The two of them existing in the same place. Each of them working on their own. Never together. The thought saddened her for some reason.

When she returned, she was surprised to see him finishing the last rung of a sloped ladder leading up to the top bunk. He'd woven deer hide strips to make a base for the top bunk then thrown his own mattress over them, creating a comfortably looking bed.

"Thank you," she said as she watched him lay out a deer hide and a blanket onto the lower bed for himself.

He grunted, picked up his hammer and started to leave, then stopped and grabbed two more biscuits before stepping outside and hanging up his tools.

She followed him only to find him starting back up the hill.

"Where are you going?" she asked as a strange feeling filled her.

He frowned at her as if she were asking the stupidest question ever asked. "To work," he said with a shake of his head. "I'm sliding behind schedule."

And that was their morning, she thought with a sinking feeling of sadness. A dozen words. And two dozen grunts. She rolled her eyes. The man   was   a   lost   cause.

Chapter Eight

Hank set down the double-jack and sighed as he examined his work. It had taken a while to muck out the rockfall from before he'd left. He'd had to use the double-jack on a few of the bigger chunks of waste rock to get them in the barrow. He'd set aside the ore bearing quartz and would drag it out in the morning. Then he could spend a day or two drilling the next set of holes.

A satisfying feeling of accomplishment filled him. His muscles felt used, sore like they should.

Sighing, he held up the lamp to examine the vein of white quartz. Six inches wide, it ran north-south at a sixty degree angle. Sandwiched between a wall of granite and gray slate. Would he ever hit the motherload? he wondered. He was getting enough color to pay. But he was having to move a ton of rock to get an ounce of gold. Not enough to make a man rich.

Moving the lamp higher, he examined the vein in the overhead. Was it richer up higher? Or maybe beneath him? That was the thing. A fortune could be within feet of him and he'd never know it.

Maybe he should run a stope up into the ceiling. It would make the rock weaker, but he could brace it with timbers.

He shook his head. There was no way of knowing. Not today anyway. Those were problems that could be solved later. For now, he needed to eat and give his body a chance to recover from a hard day of swinging his sledgehammer.

A loud clank echoed through the shaft when he pulled the drill from the hole and dropped it on the ground next to the others. Time to go back. He couldn't avoid it much longer. She wasn't going anywhere.

He ducked as he walked back down the shaft to the open air. Once he stepped outside he stood up straight for the first time in hours and twisted about to get things back in the proper place.

Then he looked down at his cabin and sighed. Smoke rose from the chimney. He wondered if she had made any more of those biscuits. She'd brought the horses back to the corral he could see. That was one task he wouldn't have to perform every day. One less thing to keep him away from the mine.

He sighed to himself as he started down the trail. What would it be like tonight? he wondered. The both of them sleeping in the same room. His stomach tightened up. He needed to get her out of here before he did something they both regretted.

The fear in her eyes whenever he was near made it so obvious. To her, he would always be a monster. Something to despise. She might need him at the moment. But that was only because she was being chased by a worse monster.

Putting it aside, he passed by the cabin to the creek below where he could dip his head in the cool water and rinse off the dust and dirt caked to him.

He laughed to himself, if there hadn't been a woman in his cabin, he'd have slapped the dirt away and washed it off next Sunday. But he imagined she wouldn't like him tracking in dirt and mud.

As he walked back to the cabin he steeled himself for a tense evening. What do people do with each other? he wondered. In the Army, it was easy. He could sit back and let the other's talk. They'd learned to not ask him questions.

But now, just the two of them. She'd want to talk.

The thought sent a shudder down his back. Oh well, best get it over with, he thought as he opened the door.

He froze. Things looked ... clean, he realized. Swept and dusted. Wildflowers sat in a canning jar in the middle of the table and he was hit with the delicious smell of cooked trout and more biscuits.

Amy was bent over by the fire stirring at the coals. She turned to look over her shoulder and he was hit with a wave of desire that shocked him. Their eyes locked for a second and he could see that she was aware of his thoughts. But she didn't turn away. Not immediately.

Finally, the both of them pulled back from their locked gaze.

"You're just in time," she said as she stood up. "I didn't know when you would come home."

He almost laughed. Home. Such a special word. But it did feel like home. Welcoming. One day and she'd made things seem easier, more comfortable.

"Sit," she said as she pulled a large frying pan off the grill. "I found some fishhooks in that tin can you keep by the sourdough mother."

His stomach clenched up.

"I saw the medal also," she said without looking at him.

He took a deep breath. "Yeah, got it in the Army."

She studied him for a long second. "Even I know that the long blue ribbon means it is a special one. It says VALOR on the front and on the back, it says 'The Congress to Private Henry Richards.' It's a Medal of Honor, isn't it?"

He pushed down the nervousness inside of him and nodded to the fish on the plate. "You going to feed me or do I need to wrestle you for it?"

She blushed prettily, then slid two golden-brown fried trout onto his plate. Then she opened a bowl of boiled greens and nudged the plate of fresh biscuits at him.

He closed his eyes and took in the savory aroma of good food.

"Are you going to tell me anything about it?" she asked, obviously referring to the medal.

"No," he said as he used his fork to dish up the greens onto his plate.

She grumbled under her breath then placed the third trout onto her own plate and sat down across from him. The two of them ate in silence for a long moment.

A man could get used to this, he thought. Coming home to a good meal. It sure beat leftover beans.

"What did you do today?" she asked.

He sighed inside. She'd dropped the whole Army subject. At least for now. But he was sure she'd work her way around to it at some point.

"Pounded hard steel into hard rocks to make small holes. That's pretty much it," he replied around a bite of the best food he'd had in ages. His insides sort of melted as he savored the explosion of flavor in his mouth.

She nodded at the beds in the corner. "I made you a mattress," she said. "I had to use grass and straw."

He froze then turned to look at the mattress she'd crafted out of old flour sacks sewn together in one long tube. It was thick and looked like it would be perfect.

"If you threw that hide over it," she added, "the straw won't poke at you." He swallowed hard then nodded. "Thank you," he said.

Her eyes opened wide at his appreciation. He almost laughed to himself. See, he wanted to say. I'm not a complete monster.

She smiled slightly. "It isn't right for a man to be uncomfortable in his own cabin," she said with a sarcastic tone.

He winced, having his own words thrown back at him hurt more than they should have. The woman knew how to hit her mark well. He pretended not to have noticed her sarcasm and instead finished his meal in silence.

As he watched her clear the dishes, he cringed inside thinking about the long evening stretching out in front of them.

"Do you know how to play cribbage?" he asked as he got up to remove the board and deck of cards from the chest.

She turned, her eyes open wide in surprise. "Yes," she said. "My father taught me."

He nodded as he removed the pegs for the board. "Good," he said. "I ain't found a good player since I worked in Virginia City. Dusty couldn't stand the game. And Jack was always too busy."

She frowned slightly. "Do you have any other friends? You mention those two a lot."

He shook his head. "None that is still living. The war took too many."

From the corner of his eye, he saw her wince and mentally kicked himself. The last thing he wanted to do was talk about the war. Especially not with her. There were too many awful memories. No. He just wanted a nice quiet evening. Something to pass the time until they could go to bed.

The thought made him swallow hard as he glanced over at the bunk beds. He'd be sleeping in a room with a beautiful woman. Young and enticing. It was going to be a troubling night. In fact, he doubted he'd get a wink of sleep. Of course, it was better than sleeping on the ground. His back couldn't take much more of that.

When she was finished washing the dishes, she sat down across from him and they began to play. He was surprised to discover just how good she was. Maneuvering him into laying just the right card at the wrong time.

It took every bit of concentration to beat her. When he'd pegged the last stop, he sat back and smiled. She looked up at him with a strange expression, then said, "Again. You got lucky."

He almost smiled when he realized just how right she was.

They played into the dark evening, both of them working hard. Rejoicing in every extra point. It was nice to find someone who understood the nuances of the game. But finally, he caught her yawning and had to admit that they couldn't put it off any longer.

"I'm going to take a walk around the place," he said as he got up and grabbed the shotgun from above the door. "I should be back in ten or fifteen minutes or so."

She swallowed hard as her face turned pale. She obviously understood that he was giving her time to get ready for bed and under the covers before he came back. As he stepped out into the darkness, he looked up at the stars above and shook his head. It was going to be a long night with troubling dreams. He just knew it.

A quick glance at the cowl around the moon sent a surge of fear through him. Winter was coming. There weren't no way to stop it. He needed to get her over the mountain or they'd be stuck here until next spring.

When he came back inside, he immediately noticed her in the upper bunk. She lay on her side, watching him. She'd let her hair down. His stomach tensed up. Something about a woman's hair spread out over a pillow could make a man rethink what was right and wrong.

Pushing the urge away, he hung up the shotgun, unlaced his boots, turned down the lamp, removed his shirt and crawled into bed. He couldn't help but smile. The woman knew how to make a mattress, that was for sure.

Folding his hands under his head he stared at the interlaced strips of hide above him. The dips indicating where her hips rested. His gut tightened with need. Who was this woman? He wondered. Sharp-witted, beautiful, in a pure, innocent way that tore at his soul. Strong, independent.

The kind of woman a man could admire.

No, he grumbled to himself as he turned over. Don't be thinking that. A few weeks and then she would be gone. No way was he going to start caring for the woman. That way only lay pain and misery.

He was a loner. A miner in the backwoods. Women didn't fit in that kind of life. Besides he wasn't exactly what a woman was looking for. Especially not a woman like Miss Amy Dunn.

Chapter Nine

Amelia finished cleaning the two rabbits Hank had shot earlier that morning. She then glanced up at the mine shaft with a burning curiosity. She'd been here for three days yet he still hadn't invited her up to the shaft to show her what he was doing.

She needed to know about him. Who was he? Why did he do what he did? Slowly a plan began to form in her mind. He couldn't complain if she brought him food.

Once she'd put together a lunch of fried rabbit and fresh sourdough bread, she started up the trail to the mine shaft. As she approached the entrance, she heard a distant steady rhythmic clank.

Taking a deep breath, she paused at the opening and looked down the long dark shaft. The first six feet were lined with heavy timbers holding up the ceiling. The rest was as rough domed tunnel stretching off into the darkness. At the far end, she could see a small flame casting strange shadows.

"Hank," she called.

There was no answer, just another heavy clank followed shortly after by another.

She swallowed and slowly entered. As she moved into the shaft, she examined the sharp jagged rocks jutting out from the wall. When she looked up above her, she shuddered thinking of all the rock overhead.

It would crush her into mush if it fell. A feeling of trepidation filled her. How did he spend all day in here without going insane? Swallowing hard, she looked behind her to make sure she could still see the entrance. It took every bit of effort to force her feet to move her toward the distant flame at the end of the shaft.

As she drew nearer, the clank sound grew louder, bouncing off the walls and echoing through her entire body.

Then she saw movement and heard another heavy clank. She continued forward, then froze when she saw him outlined in the yellow lamplight. Shirtless, his strong muscles rippled every time he swung the heavy sledgehammer.

He reminded her of a picture she'd seen once about those Roman gods. There had been one named Vulcan. All muscle, swinging a hammer, his face creased with concentration and determination.

That was Hank at that moment. He would swing the hammer against the drill bit, the clank would echo down the shaft. He'd grab the drill, twist it, then swing again. Over and over until he'd punched a hole into the hard rock.

She could only stand there and admire him as he worked. His body covered in sweat and dust, working like a smooth machine. A man designed for such duties.

As he pulled the drill from the hole he turned and saw her standing there. His face froze then turned to a heavy scowl.

"What are you doing here?" he barked.

She swallowed hard and held out the plate. "I brought you lunch."

Hank continued to scowl at her. "You don't come in here. It's not safe."

"You're here," she responded before she could stop herself. She despised being told she couldn't do something.

"That's different," he said as he took up the lantern from the shaft's floor and stepped towards her so that he could take her elbow to guide her out.

"Please," she said as she pulled away from him. "Just tell me what you're doing so I understand. You use these strange terms like stope and drift and I don't know what you're talking about. I'll never come back. Just tell me."

He sighed heavily as he took a deep breath. She had to fight not to stare at his wide chest.

"I'm punching holes either side of the vein..."

"Is that the vein?" she asked. "The white rock."

He nodded. "Yeah, the quartz. I'll blow about a two-foot deep section off the face either side of the vein. Make the opening wide enough so I can get in and drill more holes for the next section."

"Where's the gold?" she asked as she lifted his hand with the lamp to examine the heavy rock around them.

He moved the lamp to the edge of the white quartz where it met up against the gray rock. "See that red, crumbly bit on the edge of the quartz?" she nodded. "That's where the gold is, mixed in there. If I'm lucky."

She continued to frown. "I thought you could just pick it out of the rock?"

He laughed. "I should be so lucky. A miner might find a pocket like that once in his lifetime. But usually, I've got to crush the rock into a fine dust then wash it down the sluice."

Amelia studied the rock and could only shake her head at how much she didn't understand. Then she realized she was standing next to a very virile, very shirtless man. Her body quivered with awareness.

She froze, afraid to move unless she do the wrong thing. Afraid to send the wrong signals or worse, send them and be ignored. Instead, she swallowed hard and waited for him to back away.

Finally, he coughed and stepped back when he realized just how close they were.

"Go on," he said as he pointed back to the shaft's opening.

She sighed heavily and made her way back down the shaft towards the speck of light at the far end. When they stepped outside, she took in a deep breath, thankful to be out from beneath all of that rock.

"What'd you make me?" Hank asked as he blew out the lamp and sat on a big boulder just outside the mine's portal.

"Rabbit," she said as she uncovered the plate. "And fresh bread."

He smiled and her heart shifted a little. The man was still shirtless, and now, in the light of day even more powerful.

He took a bite then said in answer to her previous question, "A stope is when I dig up into the shafts ceiling. A wince is digging down through the floor. A drift is a tunnel either side."

She nodded, pleased to learn a little more.

"Where does the gold come from?" she asked. "Why is it in with the quartz?"

He paused for a second. "Don't rightly know. It just is."

Amelia's shoulders slumped she hated mysteries.

"But I got some ideas," he continued. "Spend enough time tunneling into rock. A man starts to see things. Talked to engineers and old high graders."

She watched as his eyes took on a serious expression while he looked out into the distance.

"You ever seen how rocks can be layered. I was down in the Grand Canyon area a few years ago. Them rocks layers went on forever."

Amelia nodded. She'd noticed rocks like that back in the Ozarks. She'd never really thought about it. But they'd been there.

"Well," he continued, "I figure the rocks around here were like that one time. Flat, like a cake. Then the mountains come along for some reason. Pushed them layers up into broken patterns. You can see it up in Utah. Rocks the size of farms pushed up to almost standing on end."

She watched him intently. The passion in his voice surprised her. He'd thought about this a lot she realized. Of course he had. His living depended upon it.

"Anyway. I figure them layers split and got separated. Small cracks opened up between them. And then water got in there. Maybe like them hot springs in Yellowstone..."

"You've been a lot of places," she said.

"Yeah well, never could find what I was looking for. Anyway. That water gets up in the cracks, full of minerals. The quartz crystals form like salt does when it dries out. and them metals mixed in the water settle to the bottom of the crack. That's why you find the gold in amongst the rusty iron or the pyrite. In Virginia City it's mixed in with silver mostly."

Amelia looked at him with amazement. The man was not unintelligent. He probably knew more about rocks and the land underneath them than a college professor. It was a mistake to think that because he was so big that he lacked brains.

"So, you have to crush the rock to get at the gold," she said as it finally began to make sense.

He nodded then smiled. "Of course, there are exceptions. Knew a man who pulled fifty-six pounds of pure gold out of a pocket the size of a steamer trunk after digging through six hundred yards of low-grade stuff. Saw a miner showing off a nugget the size of your fist one time in Denver. But it's rare."

Amelia stared off into the distance to keep from looking at his very large, very exposed chest and shoulders. Her mind kept drifting to thoughts no respectable woman should be having.

"The rabbit's good," he said, holding up a piece. "Maybe I'll go for a buck in the morning. There's a spot over the ridge to the west where they bed down. If I get there early enough, I might get one."

The thought of a steady supply of meat made her smile. She could do so much with it.

The two of them sat there in a comfortable silence while he finished his meal. A soft wind blew down the canyon carrying the scent of pine and sage. A hawk circled in the distance, and a soft white cloud crossed in front of the sun.

It was nice, she realized. Peaceful. A world unto itself. So unlike anything she had ever known before.

"Well," Hank said as he stood up and stretched. Her eyes couldn't help but track the way his muscles moved. "Back at it. That rock ain't going to move itself."

"Can I help?" she asked suddenly despising the idea of being left alone. There was only so much cleaning she could do. She needed something to keep her busy.

He studied her for a long moment then said, "Not today. Not really. But when it comes time to muck it out. Maybe."

Her heart soared. He hadn't dismissed her out of hand. He hadn't thought that because she was a woman she couldn't help. It was progress, she thought. Maybe there was hope for him after all.

.o0o.

Hank worked his way down from the crest of the ridge. His eyes shifted from the deer in the distance to the trail in front of him. One wrong step and he'd spook them.

As he gently placed his foot down, he glanced to find the next safe spot for his boot when his heart jumped to his throat. A moccasin track. Clear as day. Indians.

Without thinking he dropped lower as his eyes scanned the area. Once he felt secure, he examined the track. It was small. Either a boy or a woman's and there weren't much reason for an Indian woman to be up here. There weren't nothing worth collecting except pine nuts and there were a lot more of those down lower.

So, an Indian boy's track. Maybe a day old. Just because it was a boy's track didn't make it nothing to worry about. They started their warriors out pretty young.

Was this a warrior scouting out the cabin? He thought back to the prickly feeling between his shoulder blades yesterday when he walked down from the mine shaft. Had that been it? Had this boy been watching him?

It would explain the feeling. But why? It didn't make sense. Slowly, he turned and looked back up at the ridge behind him. A person could rest up there and watch the mine all day without being seen.

He shuddered thinking about Amy being watched by some stranger. Going to the creek for water. Walking up the trail to the shaft. She had been exposed. In danger. The thought ignited an anger inside of him.

Hold off, he told himself. It might just be a curious boy. Don't go flying off the handle assuming the worst.

He took a deep breath to calm himself then focused on the deer. If there were Indians in the area. There wasn't much he could do about it. There had been some problems, but not much. Not like the problems they were having down in Texas or Arizona or up in the Dakotas.

Once he had his emotions under control again, he refocused on the deer. They needed meat.

Later, with the buck across his shoulders, he made his way back up the trail, once again stopping to examine the moccasin tracks. Next to it was the mark of his big boot. Well, they'd know now that he was aware of them. It was up to them to make the next move.

When he got back the cabin, he hung the carcass from a branch and pulled his knife from his belt to sharpen it.

"I'll do that," Amy said as she stepped up to him, admiring the deer.

"You sure?" he asked.

She scoffed and shook her head. "I was raised on a farm. I bet I can dress a deer as well as you can swing a hammer."

Hank raised an eyebrow but he handed over his knife and stepped back. It took him all of a half-minute to realize she knew what she was doing.

She stopped and turned back to him, her brow furrowed. "You still got the afternoon. And that gold isn't going to walk out of that mine on its own."

He laughed and shook his head. The woman was remarkable. Beautiful, and able to skin a deer. Who would ever have guessed?

Shaking his head, he started to return his rifle to the pegs above the door but changed his mind and decided to hold onto it. That moccasin track gave him worries. Instead, he grabbed a couple of biscuits and headed up to the shaft. As he passed Amy his stomach rumbled at the thought of venison steaks for dinner.

She shot him a quick smile then returned to gutting the deer.

Hank sighed, then was struck by an urge to stay and help. The thought surprised him. Since when had he wanted to work next to someone. It wasn't in his nature. He shook off the feeling and started up to the mine.

See, that was what happened when a woman looking like her was around. A man's thoughts drifted off away from where they should be.

But, no matter how much he grumbled at himself. He still couldn't shake the feeling of what might have been. No. he needed to get her away and over the mountains before he changed his mind.

Chapter Ten

Amelia hung the last of the meat and stepped back. She'd cut out the steaks for the evening meal and set them aside. She would let the rest age a little in the larder. But she could get a week's worth of meals from it. She'd make sausage and pemmican from the rest before it went bad.

Yes, she thought with a sense of accomplishment. Life was good. Then she looked down at her bloody hands and shook her head. She needed to get cleaned up before Hank came home. She'd been careful to keep her dress clean. But her arms were atrocious.

Smiling to herself at the thought of serving him a good meal, she retrieved a flour sack, a bar of store-bought soap then started for the creek.

After washing her hands, she stood and looked at the deep blue pool. The water looked so fresh and clear. It would be so wonderful to just sink in and let it wash away weeks of dirt.

Yes, she thought as she carefully began to unbutton her dress. Hank wouldn't be back for hours and there was no one to see. If the man had a washtub she wouldn't have to resort to a cold creek. But she needed a bath. She wanted to feel clean. That bone-deep clean that a person couldn't get with a bucket and a rag.

Once out of her dress, she slipped out of her shift, then her underthings. She held her clothes next to her body as her stomach turned over with nervousness. She quickly glanced around but she was alone. As alone as a person could be.

Amelia pushed aside her nervousness as she hung her clothes up over a rock high on the bank so that they could warm in the sun. She'd be glad for their warmth when she got out of that freezing water.

Again, she looked around to make sure no one was watching before she worked her way down to a large rock at the water's edge. Taking a deep breath, she dipped in a toe before pulling it back quickly. The water was colder than a banker's heart.

She held her breath and stepped into the creek. The soft sand under her feet felt firm and safe. Her body shivered but she forced herself deeper until she could sink down and cover her shoulders. Biting back against the chill, she quickly began to wash. Determined to do a thorough job. It became a battle of wills. Who would win, Amelia or the freezing water?

The entire time, she kept shifting, searching for anyone watching. The thought of Hank finding her like this sent a different type of shiver down her back.

Once she was clean, she ignored her chattering teeth and shivering body to start on her hair. Letting it down, she used the bar of soap between dunking her head to rinse it out. Only when her fingers became too numb to hold the bar did she surrender. She swallowed hard and gave another inspection in all directions to make sure she was alone then stepped up out of the creek.

She quickly dried off, terrified at being discovered naked and exposed. She held onto the flour sack as she stepped up onto a boulder to reach for her underthings.

Maybe it was her wet feet, but she would never know why. Without warning, her foot slipped on the smooth boulder. Her arms reached for balance, the flour bag fluttering off into the wind. But she could not save herself. She fell.

Her foot slipped down between boulders as she fell backwards. Her right knee and ankle were wrenched when they got trapped in the giant boulders. Her left leg scrapped against something rough as she landed on her back with a heavy whoomph sound.

A bolt of pain shot through her entire body as she tried to breath.

"No," she cried as she fought to hold back a scream. Every part of her yelled for attention but it was her trapped leg that screamed the loudest. Gritting her teeth, she tried to pull it back, but the foot refused to move.

It felt like it was encased in a bucket of concrete. Even her toes couldn't wiggle.

A sudden panic filled her. She was hurt. Seriously hurt, and stuck. The pain was there, but she knew it would be even worse soon when the shock wore off.

She took a deep breath and tried to steady herself. Careful, she told herself. Don't panic. It would just make it worse. What about the rest of her? She quickly ran an assessment. She hadn't hit her head, that was a blessing. Her back felt sore, scraped, and bruised, but it worked. It was her legs that were the problem. The right was trapped, and the left felt like someone had scraped at the bone with a rusty knife. Reaching down, she felt something wet and sticky on the back of her thigh.

When she brought her hand up, her fingers showed blood. Oh, and to top it off, she was laying on her back next to a creek, naked as a jaybird. Other than that, she was just fine.

She twisted her head side to side as she searched for the flour sack. Anything to cover herself. But it was gone, probably floating down the creek halfway to Reno by now. She took a deep breath as she looked at her dress only a few feet away but it might as well be in Denver for all the help it was doing her.

She bit down against the pain and tried to move her trapped leg again. She needed to get free before Hank found her like this. Her stomach churned with a combination of fear and shame as she tried to use her hands to move her leg.

Nothing. It was like trying to pull a tree out of the ground. That leg wasn't going to move.

Suddenly, she thought about the wild animals in the area. She was defenseless. Or what if the creek rose. A sudden storm up in the hills. Her head was only inches from the rushing water.

A new cold fear filled her. She could die here, or worse, Hank could discover her like this. She'd die of shame.

Frustration washed through her. She had been such a fool. A misplaced step. Why had she hung her clothes out of reach? Idiotic, to say the least.

As she bit down against the pain flowing through her, she heard a distant rumble and felt the ground shiver beneath her. Hank had set off the charge, she realized. He would be coming home soon. He always blew the charges at the end of the day so the dust could settle overnight before he went in and mucked out the rock.

Her heart pounded in her chest as she realized he would come looking for her. The man was too much a hero at heart to ever let her be in danger. He'd take one look at the deer carcass and realize she'd come down to the creek to wash.

The idiot. He was going to come after her. She just knew it.

Once again, she tried to pull her leg free, twisting and fighting against the pain. But it was no good. She wasn't moving. Sighing heavily, she laid back and tried to regain her breath.

What if he didn't come? she thought with a sudden fear. What if he thought she'd left? The man would probably whoop with joy, she thought with a snort.

No, he would come. Her life wouldn't work out any other way. And he'd probably laugh at her stupidity. She could well imagine it. Him seeing her naked and laughing. It sent a new fear through her.

Taking a deep breath, she laid back and tried to gather herself for another try. She needed to get free. It was her only chance.

As she lay there taking deep breaths, she closed her eyes and tried to forget the pain. Think of something good, she told herself. But the vision of Hank working shirtless in his mine kept flashing into her brain.

She bit the inside of her cheek against the pain. Anything to distract her when a shadow passed over her, making her eyes spring open.

There on the bank was Hank, looking down at her with a strange look to his eyes.

She squealed and immediately covered herself with her hands. He turned away to give her some privacy.

"You all right?" he asked.

"Of course, I am. I prefer to trap my leg and lie in the sun like this," she snapped out.

"In that case, I'll leave you to it," he said with a chuckle as he turned away.

"Don't you dare," she yelled.

His smile made her angry but he turned back to her and started to climb down.

"Stay there," she hissed.

He froze then shrugged his shoulders. "You're choice. I'll just stay here all day. I got to admit, the view is as pretty as a polished nugget. Don't know that I seen any better."

Her insides tensed up. The man was enjoying this. The beast. Couldn't he see how unfair this was? How humiliating. Then it hit her. Of course not. All he could see was a naked woman laying on a rock.

"My foot's trapped," she said as she started to point to the big boulder then realized her mistake and quickly covered herself again.

He nodded as he jumped down the rest of the way and peered down into the crack between the rocks.

"My dress," she said to him. "Please."

He shrugged his shoulders. "If you insist." Reaching up he moved her underthings and retrieved her dress. She felt her body flush with shame. But he didn't comment, instead, he gently laid the dress over her.

Amelia instantly grabbed the fabric to hold it around her. Yes, she thought, she was armored again. No longer vulnerable.

"How did this happen?" he asked as he reached down and tried to free her foot.

She winced sharply at his cold hand and the pain that shot up her leg.

Hank backed off and studied the rocks then turned, put a foot on either side of her hip and his back against the giant boulder.

"You can't move that," she said.

He frowned at her. "Told you before. Don't tell me I can't do something."

She almost laughed. That was exactly what she needed. Him determined to do the impossible.

As he began to strain against the rock his face became red. The veins on his temple stood out with the effort as he grunted and heaved with all his might.

She watched, amazed at him for even trying. No single man could move that rock. Then, as if in answer to her prayers, the giant boulder began to move. Her foot could wiggle just a little. Hank grunted short breaths as he put every ounce of his being into moving the rock.

"NOW," he yelled as the rock shifted up off her foot.

Amelia pulled it free as she scooted back, being sure to keep her dress as a cover.

Hank grunted one last time then let the rock fall back into place with a cracking snap sound. He stood there, his legs on either side of her, looking down with a serious expression that confused her.

Then, as if remembering where he was, he shifted to pick her up like she was a newborn kitten. Amelia felt herself lifted with ease. Of course, it was easy, she thought, the man had just shifted two tons of rock.

He scrambled up the bank with her in his arms like a mountain goat. As they passed her clothes she reached out and grabbed her shift and underthings, immediately sliding them under her dress to hide them.

She felt him laugh as his chest moved with a deep chuckle. His chest was as hard as granite as he held her next to him while he made his way up the trail to the cabin. When he shifted to get between two trees, she looked up at him. Amazed at the feeling of security she felt in his arms. It was as if she was protected from every bad thing in the world.

His square jaw was covered in two days of beard. He had shaved it on Sunday. His brow was furrowed for some reason. It couldn't be the strain of carrying her. The man had carried a pack weighing more than she did for a dozen miles uphill.

No, it wasn't the strain that had caused that strange look in his eyes.

"That leg looks pretty bad," he said as he approached the cabin. "I guess that means I'll have to cook my own dinner."

She gasped until she saw him wink at her with a smile.

He might be a monster, she thought. But there were times when having a monster around came in handy.

Chapter Eleven

Hank gently laid her on his bed and stepped back as a sense of relief washed through him. He'd been worried when he'd found her missing. Then shocked to discover her lying like that by the creek.

At first, he'd thought she was simply sunning herself dry and he'd been unable to look away. It was wrong. But he couldn't not look. The woman was beautiful. With all the most perfect curves. Even now, it was impossible to get that picture out of his mind.

He took a deep breath and stepped away from the bed. She looked up at him with blushing cheeks, obviously embarrassed at what he had seen.

"I'm going to have to look at that foot and that cut on your other leg,"

She swallowed and grabbed at the dress covering her. The look of terror in her eyes told him she still didn't trust him. She probably never would. And really, he couldn't blame her. If she knew the thoughts running through his mind half the time she'd run for the hills even if she had to hop on one foot the whole way.

He turned away to give her a moment and started cutting flour sacks into long bandages then pulled out a small pot of salve from the bottom of his chest. Miss Consuela had given it to him the last time he'd been out at Dusty and Rebecca's ranch.

When he lifted the lid, he winced. The stuff smelled like a wet sock hidden in a hole for a hot summer. Dusty swore by it though. Hank could only hope it worked. He didn't have much choice.

Once he had things set up on the table, he got a bucket of water from the rain barrel and approached the bed. He raised an eyebrow, waiting for her to accept the inevitable. "Ain't no need to be modest. I done seen everything there is to see."

"Hank," she gasped as her cheeks flushed full red.

He cussed to himself inside. He was such an idiot. She was a woman. Not one of his Army buddies.

Amy watched him with an intense stare like he was a snake ready to strike. He could only wait until she finally sighed and slowly pulled up the hem of her dress to expose her ankles and calf.

He took a deep breath and focused on his task. But it was such a fine ankle. A man could forget about the rest of the world. Even swollen and bruised, it was most fine.

As he gently probed, he watched her face for some indication as to the level of pain. She bit her lip as she shifted up onto her elbows so she could watch him work.

"I don't think it's broken," he told her finally. "And your knee's a little swollen, but not too bad."

She nodded as she continued to bite her lip while he wrapped the ankle in a figure eight to give it support. When he was done, he gently laid the leg back onto the bed. Now came the embarrassing part.

Her face grew even redder as she took a deep breath and pulled the dress up to the top of her thigh.

Hank froze for a moment then swallowed hard. When he glanced at her he found her watching him with a strange look. As if she expected him to attack her there in the bed.

"Like I said," he said as he wrung out the cloth. "You ain't my type." The words had no sooner left his mouth when he knew he was lying through his teeth. The woman was everyman's dream. But maybe if she thought he wasn't interested she might trust him a little more. At least enough for him to do what needed to be done.

She frowned and almost looked mad for a brief second then said, "Just hurry up."

"Knew a nurse once, in a field hospital," Hank said as he leaned across her to gently wash the wound. "She said that the best medicine was a bar of soap. That keeping wounds clean saved more men than any surgeon."

"What was her name?" Amy asked him through clenched teeth.

His heart ached hurting her like this but it was important. And if they talked, maybe it would keep her mind off the pain.

"Kathleen," he said as he gently applied the salve to the wound. Oh Kathleen, he thought with a smile.

"You were sweet on her," she said with surprise as her nose scrunched up when she got a whiff of the salve.

He paused for a moment then shrugged. "Every man who went through that hospital was sweet on her."

She studied him for a moment with a curious frown. "No. There was more. She was sweet on you as well I bet."

Again, he shrugged. How had they gotten into this conversation? Here he was trying to help her and it was costing him stories that he didn't want to talk about.

"What happened to her?" Amy asked.

He swore the woman was like a terrier after a rat. She wouldn't let go. He sighed heavily. "She married a doctor like any intelligent woman would. I heard they moved to upstate Vermont after the war. Probably got a passel of kids by now."

Amy frowned then reached out to touch his arm. "I'm sorry."

He snorted and shook his head. "Ain't no never mind. Like I said. I ain't got time for a wife."

"Or a mistress," Amy added with a small laugh.

He paused as he started to fold a bandage to place over the salve. "Do you really want to be talking about mistresses at a time like this?"

She blanched, then blushed again and shook her head.

Hank laughed to himself. That had shut her up. Now the hard part. He held the wrapping bandage in place then raised an eyebrow at her.

Amy bit her lip, made sure the dress still covered the important parts, then lifted her leg so he could get the wrap around it. Neither of them talked. Neither even admitted the other existed. It was as if they pretended this wasn't awkward then they could get through it.

When he tied off the bandage, he stood and backed off. She immediately pulled down her dress to cover herself and looked at him with a fearful expression.

"Can we just pretend this never happened?" she asked him. "That you didn't find me out there like … like that?"

He laughed. "Sure, we can pretend all you want. But that don't mean I can pretend away the picture in my mind."

"You really are a beast," she grumbled.

"Never said otherwise," he chuckled as he took up the bucket and started to leave. At the door, he looked back at her. He really wasn't going to be able to get the picture of her lying naked on that rock out of his mind. He was almost sure it would be the last thought he had in this life.

"You can get dressed," he told her. "But stay in bed. I don't need you falling and hurting yourself worse."

She shot him an angry look, but she didn't argue. He had to give her that. The woman knew when she couldn't win an argument. No, she'd keep her powder dry for another fight some other time.

.oOo.

Amelia felt as if she'd never recover from the shame and embarrassment. He'd found her naked. Then, to make matters worse. He'd carried her home. She could still remember the feel of her bare legs resting in his strong arms.

Then, in the cringe worthy moment of all time. He'd wrapped that bandage around her thigh. His hands had been surprisingly tender. Almost as if he cared enough to be worried about hurting her. It had seemed so intimate while also embarrassing.

How could she ever look him in the face again? How could she live with him in the same house? Every time she saw him, she would know what he was thinking.

A stomach churning, shame filled her.

Yet he'd treated her as if she were nothing but a pet kitten in need of mending. Something too stupid to take care of its self.

The man was insufferable. That was the word. Both indomitable and insufferable. A hard combination for a woman to deal with.

"Get dressed," she cursed at herself as she swung her legs over the side of the bed. The man would be back at any moment. She winced with pain as she tenderly placed weight on the injured ankle. A bolt of pain shot up through her spine.

Gritting her teeth, she held onto the bed frame with one hand while using the other to slip into her underthings and then her dress, all while keeping her foot several inches above the floor. Only when she was fully covered did she feel almost normal. Yet, things were different on so many levels.

He had said he couldn't get the picture of her out of his mind. Was that a good thing? she wondered. She'd seen the look in his eyes. He'd liked what he saw. Of that, there was no doubt in her mind. A woman could tell.

But there were things she'd never forget as well. The way he'd used his massive strength to move that rock to free her. The way it felt to be held in his arms like a precious treasure. The tenderness in his touch on her thigh.

No, things had changed.

"Not everything," she mumbled to herself as she hopped to the closest chair. He'd ordered her to stay in bed, but she refused to be dictated to. She wasn't his to order about. Besides, the thought of laying in his bed did something to her insides. It smelled like him, leather, woodsmoke, and gunpowder.

When he stepped back inside his brow furrowed in confusion when he saw her disobeying his order by sitting in a chair.

He grunted and shook his head but wisely decided not to fight her on the subject. Instead, he lifted up a crutch. To her amazement, he'd split a sapling, wrapped the bottom fourth in rawhide, lashed a brace in the middle for her hand and crossbar for under her arm.

"Thank you," she said with shock as he handed it to her.

He shook his head. "This don't mean you're supposed to be up and about. You got to give it time."

She snorted, "If you twisted your ankle would it stop you from working."

He scoffed back at her. "I ain't a slip of a girl."

"No," she said. "You're a half giant. Which means you'd be putting even more weight on that ankle."

All he could do was grumble as he rolled his eyes and walked to the fireplace.

"I'm making dinner," he said as he started snapping kindling. "Took the deer's carcass out a way for the critters. You done good hanging the meat in the larder. Ain't nothing going to get in after it in there."

She could only stare in surprise at his large back as he bent over the fire. The man had shifted to a safe subject. No mention of her embarrassment. No teasing. Had he truly forgotten it? Or was it just possible he was being kind?

No, that was impossible, she realized. He must have forgotten.

Standing, she leaned on the crutch. It worked, she thought in surprise. She could move about without hopping.

He looked over his shoulder and frowned. "Just sit down. You can go gallivanting about tomorrow."

She frowned back at him as she stood there in defiance.

He sighed heavily. "Please," he said. "Otherwise I'm going to have to stop cooking and follow you around to catch you, and I'm hungry."

Her insides melted. The man had said please. Really, she didn't need to make his life more difficult. Once again, he had saved her, and she was repaying him by acting like a child. She bit back a heavy sigh and sat down where she could watch him work over the fire.

117

"I'll sit down, only because you asked so nicely. But I'm not laying on your bed and I'm not ready to climb up into mine."

He nodded. "When it comes time, I'll lift you up there. Ladders ain't easy to hop on."

She swallowed hard as her cheeks grew very warm. The thought of his hands on her waist sent a thrill through her entire body.

Later, when he dished up a meal of venison steaks, and beans cooked with salt pork. She took a bite and smiled at him. It was good.

"Don't act too surprised," he said as he cut into his steak. "I been cooking for myself for years."

"I didn't say a thing."

He smiled slightly. "But, you was thinking it. No woman likes to believe a man can cook. Sort of upsets the normal balance of things."

She laughed as she took another bite. This was nice. They were talking about things other than her embarrassment earlier that afternoon. Then she saw it in his eyes. A brief memory flashed behind his eyes and she knew he was thinking about those pictures in his head.

"I wouldn't worry too much," Hank said to her. "That ankle should be good as new before we head to Sacramento. Got to give Simmons time to forget about you."

Her insides curled up. The man couldn't wait to be rid of her.

Chapter Twelve

Amy woke to a dull pain radiating up her leg. The memory of what she had come to call 'her embarrassment' flooded back into her mind. That memory was followed by the memory of his tender fingers washing her wound.

"Made you some willow bark tea," Hank called to her from the fireplace. "Should have done it last night."

She swallowed hard as she forced herself to sit up in bed.

"You want me to lift you down or you want to try the ladder?" he asked.

The memory of his strong hands holding her waist as he lifted her into the upper bunk washed through her. That special tingle that had for a short moment replaced the pain.

"The ladder," she said quickly. If he touched her again, she might crumble into him and never want to leave. No, it was better this way. He was going to take her to Sacramento and she would never see him again.

The thought filled her with a sudden sadness. Why? Wasn't that what she wanted from him? Yet the thought of leaving this place filled her with a melancholy. No, it was the thought of leaving him, she realized.

The man's a beast, she reminded herself. Not fit company. Yet, deep inside she would miss him.

"Breakfast is on the table," he said. "I've had mine. You going to be all right?"

She had kept him from his work. Sighing to herself she couldn't help but admit that she was a constant bother to him. No wonder he wanted to be rid of her as fast as possible.

"Yes," she said as she worked her way down the ladder. Her ankle screamed in pain. As she climbed down, she could feel him watching her, his eyes on her hips. Ready to spring into action if she needed it. As she hobbled to the table, she was surprised to see the canning jar filled with new colorful wildflowers. Reds, purples and yellows.

He sheepishly looked away and she could almost swear he was blushing.

"I know how you set store by them," he said. "You can get the next bunch when you're able to walk like a normal person."

She winced at his sharp words then realized, he was just being curt because he was embarrassed. He'd done something nice and he hated anyone noticing. Well, the man was going to have to learn. She balanced with her crutch with one hand while she reached up to pull him down so she could kiss him on the cheek.

"Thank you," she said. "for the flowers, and for saving me yesterday."

Now she knew he was blushing, the pink in his cheeks couldn't be denied.

"Had to hike halfway to Tahoe," he grumbled as he turned away.

Amelia laughed. "There's a patch behind the shed. More flowers than you could ever need."

Again, he grumbled under his breath. She was about to tell him that if he had put water in the jar they would last longer, but she bit her tongue. No, she needed to accept the kind gesture for what it was.

"You stay off that foot," he told her. "And I'll check the bandage when I get home."

She cringed inside as she thought about him once again examining such an intimate part of her. But again, kept silent. She'd deal with that issue when she had to.

He gave her a quick nod and grabbed his rifle from above the door.

"Are you going hunting?" she asked.

He shook his head. "Saw Indian sign the other day."

She gasped as she thought about all the stories she had heard. It had never really occurred to her but of course, they were in Indian country.

"Nothing to worry about," he said trying to reassure her.

"If not, then why are you taking the rifle?"

He sighed heavily then his shoulders slumped in defeat as he scoffed. "You are too smart for your own good sometimes."

Amelia basked in the praise.

"That ain't necessarily a good thing in a woman," he added.

Her eyes opened wide until she saw the teasing smile before he turned and left. It was only later that she realized he hadn't answered her question.

For the next two days, Amelia hobbled about on the crutch as she fought the frustration and pain. She submitted to letting Hank examine her wounds each night. She always expected him to make some comment. But each time he acted as if it were of no importance. As if seeing her bare legs made no difference to him at all.

One more thing to be frustrated about, she thought with a shake of her head.

Two days. And even before that, she had been bored. It was even worse now. There wasn't enough to do. The man didn't have a farm with all the animals to help take care of. No butter to churn or chickens to feed.

No, he had a mine, she thought to herself. If she was going to keep busy, it would have to be at the mine. She grabbed Charlie's boots and laced them up tight. They will help keep her foot secure, she thought as she took up her crutch in a tight grip and started slowly hobbling her way up the trail.

As she approached, she worked her way behind a tree so she could watch and make sure she wasn't bothering him at a critical moment. She knew he was mucking out the mine from last night's blast. He should be out in a minute she told herself as she held steady behind the tree.

She'd judge his mood then decide whether to approach or not. Her ankle reminded her that this might not have been the smartest move and she was thinking of going back when she heard a rattle inside the mine followed by a shirtless Hank pushing a wooden wheelbarrow out and tipping the rocks down the front of the pile.

The other day he had explained that the waste rock was taken to the end of the tailings and dumped. The gold-bearing ore was tipped to the side for crushing. This must be ore, she realized. Her second thought was that there was something about a well-formed man using his muscles for hard physical work. Something that pulled at the female part of her.

"I know you're there, Amy," he said as he stood up straight and stretched his shoulders.

Her heart lurched. "How?" she asked as she hobbled out from behind the tree.

The big man laughed and shook his head. "Could smell you before I left the mine. Wind's behind you."

She frowned up at him.

"Soap, plus you baked this morning. And picked new wildflowers I bet. It's a woman's smell. A good one."

Her insides relaxed. He wasn't yelling at her. That was something.

"I'm bored," she said with a huff. She knew she was sounding childish but she couldn't stop herself. "Is there anything I can do?"

She held her breath while he looked out into the distance then shrugged his shoulders. "Come on," he said as he indicated the boulder just outside the entrance.

As she worked her way up the hill her heart jumped with happiness. Even if she just sat and watched him. It would be a huge improvement to her day.

Once she was seated, he took up his huge double-jack sledgehammer and gave her a quick glance to make sure she was out of the way then lifted it over his shoulder and brought it down with a mighty crack. The white rock shattered into a dozen pieces.

"I'll break them into manageable size then you can turn them into dust," he told her.

"Really?" she asked in surprise. "You're going to let me help."

He laughed and nodded. "I can't stand being bored either. Drives me to do stupid things."

She could only sit there with a secret glee watching him work. It was so much better in the daylight, she thought to herself.

When he had finished creating fist-size rocks out of the big chunks, he stepped back and pulled a bandana from his back pocket to wipe his brow. "Now It's your turn," he said as he brought a huge piece of gray flat granite and dropped it next to the ore pile. Obviously, the flat stone was to be used as an anvil.

"What do I do?"

"Use this," he said as he handed her a small, single-jack hammer. The tool was surprisingly heavy and almost dragged her to the ground.

"You can sit here on the ground. It's a one-handed hammer for tight spots in the mineshaft. But you can use two hands. Let its weight do the work for you."

She swallowed hard as she realized that he really expected her to do this. "What if …"

"You can't make it worse," he told her. "Anything you don't do, I will. When you're done, I'll get all the dirt and dust and run it through the sluice."

He was right, she realized. She couldn't break anything. In fact, it was the opposite. He wanted here to break things. But what was important was that she actually felt like she was helping.

She used her crutch to lower herself to the ground and placed a piece of rock on the granite slab, glanced up at Hank who nodded for her to try. She took a deep breath and lifted the heavy hammer before bringing it down on the quartz.

The rock only cracked. It didn't crumble into dust like when he did it.

"You'll get the hang of it," he told her as he turned to walk back into the mine. Her mouth dropped open. He was leaving her alone to do this. Did he just assume she would fail? She would show him, she thought with a sense of determination.

As she worked, she smiled to herself as the rocks began to get smaller and smaller until a few had become nothing but sand and dust.

Of course, while she worked, she examined each rock for any sign of gold. She so wanted to see it in its natural form. But it was just white quartz with a rusty red streak an inch or two wide.

Each time he pushed out a barrow of waste rock to the end of the tailings, he would glance over at her and nod with encouragement and she'd refocus, determined to do a good job. After his fifth load, he put on his shirt and sat down next to her then gently took the hammer out of her hand.

"You've done good," he told her. "Saved me a bit of work. But let me finish it up."

Amelia sighed with relief. Her shoulders were killing her. The hammer had gotten heavier and heavier with each rock. Somehow, she forced herself up onto her crutch and hobbled back to the boulder and sat down.

It seemed within minutes he'd finished the pile of ore and shoveled the dusty sand into two buckets. Without a word, he started down the trail. She hopped up to limp after him. He walked right past the cabin to the creek.

Her heart lurched. They would pass the blue pool and the place of her embarrassment. But thankfully, he kept his thoughts to himself and approached his sluice. She stood there and watched as he lifted the blocking piece of wood in the end. Immediately, water began to rush down the long wooden trough.

"These catch the gold," he said as he pointed out skinny strips of wood across the sluice's bottom. "Gold is heavy. It don't want to move. The first chance it gets it sinks. The trick is having the right amount of water. Too much, and it washes away. Too little and there's too much sand and I got to pan it out by hand which kills a day."

She could only nod, secretly ecstatic that he was taking the time to explain all of this to her.

He lifted the barrel of crushed ore and dribbled out its sand and dirt into the up creek end of the sluice. He waited for it to begin washing down the trough, then dribbled out some more. He did that for almost a half-hour until the last of the dirt was gone, tapping the barrels on the sluice's side to get the last little bit.

"There you go," he said pointing down into the sluice.

Amelia stepped forward and gasped. There along each stringer, was a line of bright gold.

"We did that?" she asked in surprise.

"Sure did," he said as he replaced the block to stop the water flowing. "This is my favorite part," he added as he used his fingers to scrape out the gold and add it to the leather pouch he pulled from his pocket.

"How much is that?" she asked.

He thought for a moment. "Maybe five, ten, dollars. A good day."

Two weeks wages she thought. A man was lucky to make a dollar a day. It was hard to believe.

"It ain't always this good," he told her as he grabbed the empty buckets and pointed up the hill to the cabin. "You bought me some luck."

She smiled to herself as she started working her way up the hill. She was a gold miner. Who would ever have believed it?

Chapter Thirteen

Hank lit the fuse then turned to hurry out of the shaft. Once outside, he stepped to the side of the shaft portal and waited. This new safety fuse worked pretty good. There hadn't been a misfire since he'd started using it. As he counted down the seconds, he looked down the hill at the cabin.

He'd insisted she stay down there when he was blasting. He smiled to himself. If she had her way, she'd be setting charges like a seasoned powderman.

A cool breeze sent a shiver down his spine. Winter was coming, he thought with trepidation. He needed to get her across the mountains before the snows set in. The thought troubled him. He'd grown to like having her there. Her smile when he came home. Her determination to help. Those saucy hips. A man could grow to enjoy her company.

The loud explosion startled him as a cloud of dust shot out of the mine. He'd lost track of time while thinking about Amy. Not a good sign. A man could get killed that way.

He shook off the thought and grabbed his rifle with one hand, and the double-jack and shovel with the other before starting down the trail to the cabin. He'd almost reached the yard just outside the cabin when he froze. There in the middle of the trail stood an Indian boy with a small game bow and three arrows in one hand and a glistening knife tied to his belt.

He wore a loose blue cotton shirt over a loincloth and calf-length moccasins with fringe around the top. At about fourteen maybe fifteen, the boy didn't offer much of a threat. But where there was one Indian there were often others.

Hank held his breath as he scanned the area but could see nothing. Next, he glanced at the cabin as his heart jumped in his chest. Amy? Was she safe?

He'd been buried deep in the tunnel. Anything could have happened and he wouldn't have known. Cursing himself, he gripped his hammer tightly as he glared at the boy. If they'd hurt her he'd tear them apart.

The boy glanced across at the cabin then back at him. Hank's gut tightened.

"Men will come for her," the boy said.

Hank rocked back in surprise. The boy spoke the white man's language. And he spoke of Amy as if he knew her.

"I spend two winters at your school," the boy said as if in answer to Hank's questioning stare. "You are the man who takes the yellow rock from the mountains. They say she might be with you."

All Hank could do was nod, this was too strange. He frantically cast about for any sign of danger. Surely this boy hadn't approached him on his own.

"White men come to my village," the boy continued. "They talk of a giant who takes woman from them."

"What's your name?" Hank demanded.

The boy frowned for a moment. Hank had heard that some Indians didn't like giving their names. They believed knowing such a thing gave another person too much power. He watched as the boy fought with himself.

"I am called Sonomma, by some in my tribe," he said finally. "Gray Jay in your words."

Hank frowned at him, "Did your father send you? Your chief? Can I talk to them?"

The boy stood up a little straighter. "I am a Paiute warrior, I come alone," the boy said. "Our chief says we are not to ... travel in your world. But I come."

"Why do you come? A chief's words should be respected." Hank asked as he looked over the boy's head for any sign of company. He was tempted to drop his tools and jack a round into the rifle. But if there were warriors hiding in the trees, a wrong move could get him filled with arrows from a dozen different directions.

The boy didn't answer. Hank pulled his gaze back down from the distant area to look directly at the boy. It took only a moment for Hank to realize the boy was embarrassed. Then it hit him. Boys were the same the world over. A pretty girl.

"She is my woman," Hank said before he could stop himself.

The boy frowned up at him. "She does not act as your woman. The men say you stole her in the night."

Hank grumbled under his breath. He didn't need to get into an argument with some boy about Amy. He was about to tell him to go home to his people when a new sound sent a shiver down his spine.

The latch to the cabin door had been thrown. "Hank, who you talking to?" Amy asked as she stepped out of the cabin.

Hank swallowed hard as his muscles bunched. Ready to fight, if the boy made a move to her or his friends rushed in. He'd take as many as he could before they got him.

Amy's eyes grew big when she saw the Indian boy. She quickly glanced at Hank to silently ask what she should do. Then looking back at the boy, she smiled slightly and said, "Hello."

The boy stared at her for a long moment then turned and disappeared into the trees.

"What …" Amy began but Hank held up a hand to stop her as he quickly scanned the area for any threat. Only when he was satisfied did his shoulders slump in relief. "It appears you've got an admirer."

She swallowed hard. "What did you tell him?"

Hank grumbled as he hung his tools on the outside cabin wall. "Told him you were my woman."

"WHAT?" she demanded as her face turned white.

He laughed. "He don't need to know the truth. Maybe it will make him keep his distance."

She looked strangely at him then followed him into the cabin. "He's a boy."

Hank shrugged his shoulders as he hung up his rifle. "The line between boy and man ain't firm. Especially not out here."

Her brow furrowed as she stared down at the floor. Obviously trying to understand the working of the male mind. Hank shook his head. It weren't that hard. Pretty woman. 'nough said. "I wouldn't be bathing down by the creek anymore," he told her with a faint smile.

Her face drained of color. "He was watching?" she said as her face shifted over to full-on red.

Hank shrugged then sat down at the table. "Dinner ready?" he asked. The sooner he changed the subject the better. But in the back of his mind was the boy's words about men coming for Amy. A sick, gut-churning fear filled him. He must get her out of here before they arrived. It was her only chance.

.o0o.

As Amelia cleared the dishes after dinner, she tried to understand what had happened. Hank had been quiet throughout the meal. She'd tried to draw him out but he'd returned to his wounded bear mode. Quiet and grumbly.

She wondered if they would play cribbage tonight. Maybe that would lighten his mood. She wanted to talk about the Indian boy. Really, she wanted to hear more about Hank declaring that she was his woman. When he had told her that her heart had jumped only to be cast down again when he explained it was all a ruse.

Yet her reaction had been a surprise to her. The sense of joy that had momentarily filled her was an indication of her true feelings, she realized. She had come to care for this man much more than she would ever have expected.

He was gruff, almost rude at times. He was tougher than boot leather and bigger than the outdoors. Her insides tightened up when she thought about just how big he was. It was like standing next to a solid rock cliff. All muscle and bone. More man than any woman could ever handle.

But, there was more. Times when he had been tender. Letting her share in his work. The flowers. The way his gentle fingers treated her wounds. The way he worked so hard. Always without complaint. The joy he got out of playing cribbage and the way he treated her when she won. It was almost as if he liked it when she did well. An unusual aspect when compared to most men.

No, there was much to admire about Hank Richards. Of course, she had been thrilled to be thought of as his woman. Even in the untruth, he was not being possessive. More protective like.

And then there was the way she had felt in his arms when he had carried her up from the creek. He had repeatedly rescued her all without making any demands. Her insides turned over as her heart raced.

What if he did make demands? Would she resist? The thought of possibly not resisting surprised her to her very core.

"Cribbage?" she asked as she fought to control the thoughts racing through her mind.

"In a second," he said as he pulled out his gold pouch and poured the yellow dust and nuggets onto a plate in the middle of the table. Amelia froze. Two weeks-worth of work. He had never done this before. Her brow furrowed as she watched him carefully divide the small hill of gold into four separate piles.

"They even?" he asked her with a serious frown.

She nodded. "Yes, I believe so."

He grunted his agreement then got up and opened his chest. He brought out the cribbage board, cards. And a small leather purse.

"Made this the other day," he said as he tossed the bag onto the table in front of her.

She picked it up to examine the four-inch leather bag with a rawhide purse string. She gasped when she saw the large A carved into the leather. He had made this for her, she realized. Why? When? Had he done this instead of working in the mine? Her heart melted as she imagined his large hands working with the soft leather.

"Thank you," she said with a hesitation as she tried to understand why he had done it.

He glanced at her then sat back down and pulled the pan of golden piles to him. "One share goes to the mine for supplies," he said as he used a playing card to scoop up a pile of gold to pour it into his own bag. "One goes for future investments. The mine is going to need a stamp mill at some point. They cost a pretty penny."

She nodded as if she understood.

"And one share for me," he said with a small smile as he tipped the third pile into his bag.

Amelia continued to watch as she tried to understand. Maybe it was some mining custom. Maybe some kind of superstition. Heaven knew men who went underground every day had reason for superstitions.

He scooped up the last pile and used his finger to make sure every stray piece of dust had been captured. "Open your bag," he said as he gave her a serious stare.

"What?" she asked. "Why?"

"Your share," he said as he indicated for her to hurry up.

Amelia gasped. No. this wasn't right.

"Come on, Amy. I don't got all night," he said with exasperation.

"I can't … You can't," she said as she gripped the purse in both hands. "It isn't right. It's not my mine. You did all the work."

He snorted as he reached over and took the bag from her hand. "You earned it." He snapped as he poured the gold into the bag and pulled the drawstring tight before giving it back to her.

Amelia stared down at the purse in her hand while he started to set up the cribbage board.

"I can't Hank," she said as she started to give the bag back.

He sighed heavily and shook his head. "I was worried you'd give me a hard time. Let me do this my way. It ain't much. Maybe fifty dollars."

Amelia froze. Fifty dollars. She didn't know if she'd ever held that much money at one time in her entire life.

"You're going to need it when you get to Sacramento," he continued. "A woman without money is too vulnerable and I won't be there to pull you out of trouble."

Her heart fell. Holding her breath, she said, "We're going to Sacramento soon?"

He   nodded,   "Tomorrow."

Chapter Fourteen

Amelia felt as if someone had punched her in the stomach.

"Tomorrow?" she whispered unable to process the thousand emotions flowing through her. He was taking her away.

He frowned as he studied her for a moment. "I've got to get you over there before the snow flies. Even more. I got to get back. If the pass gets closed, I could be stuck over there for weeks. Maybe a month or more."

Of course. His stupid mine. That was what he was worried about. Nothing could be allowed to interfere with his mine.

"You're walking pretty good now," he said as if that was her true concern. "At least when you wear Charlie's boots. And your wound didn't get infected. Consuela's salve worked. So, I think we can do it if you ride Big Bay. I'll lead Old Ben. We'll need to pack enough for about ten days. Six over. Four back for me."

She could only stare at him as she tried to listen to what he was saying. But all she could think of was that he wanted to get rid of her. A sadness filled her. She had been so stupid. How could she have ever imagined it would be any other way.

He looked at her strangely and she realized there was something he wasn't telling her.

"What else?" she asked.

He sighed heavily. "The boy said that there were men looking for you. They described a big man who took you in the night."

"That's why," she said. "It's not because you've grown tired of me. I'm not a bother."

He laughed. "Amy, you've been bothering me since the moment I stomped those two men. But it ain't your fault. A beautiful woman just naturally bothers a man."

Her heart soared. He thought she was beautiful. No one had ever said that to her before. Not like that. She sighed inside. A woman could hear words like that all her life and die a happy woman.

"Maybe they won't find us," she said as she desperately tried to think of some way to hold off the inevitable. "Didn't you say there was a danger of us being on the trail."

He nodded. "Can't put it off or you'll be stuck here all winter. We'll sneak through Truckee at night. No way they can watch the road day and night."

Her stomach clenched. Should she tell him that the idea of being stuck with him in this cabin all winter was not so terrifying to her? In fact, she realized, it sounded like the most beautiful way to spend a winter.

No, she realized. She couldn't tell him that. He was set on being free of her. Wasn't that one of the reasons he'd given her a share of his gold? It was a way to relieve his guilt.

He needn't have bothered. He had nothing to feel guilty about. If not for him she would have been trapped in a Reno brothel. No, she would always appreciate all he had done for her. Even now. He was taking time away from his mine because he was concerned for her well-being.

A sense of shame washed over her. She owed him so much. To expect more from him seemed selfish.

"I will miss our cribbage games," she told him. Her way of letting him know that she had accepted his plan.

He studied her for a moment with a strange look then took a deep breath and nodded. For just a moment she wondered if he would miss her as much as she would miss him.

Later that night, as she lay in the dark, she listened to the creek gurgling in the distance and his gentle snore from below. Her heart ached as a sole tear slowly ran down her cheek. She loved him, she realized. She truly did. But there was nothing she could do about it. No, she told herself. The mine shaft up on the hill was his true love. It always would be. No woman could compete with the thrill and danger of mining for gold. It was who he was and she would never change him.

The realization settled through her as she accepted the heartache. She turned over and tried to sleep. It was going to be a long day tomorrow. But sleep eluded her. Like a prisoner's last night before the noose. She feared missing anything as she relived every moment of their life together.

The singing birds surprised her. She had fallen asleep somehow. A sense of loss filled her as she rose to face a hard day. The bird's sweet song made her curse under her breath. They sounded too happy for such a terrible day.

Hank was already up and out the door. She cringed inside. The light under the shutter told her that she'd overslept. No wonder he wanted to be rid of her.

He'd placed her carpetbag on the table for her to pack. A gentle reminder. She sighed heavily and got down from the upper bunk. When she returning from a quick trip to the outhouse, Hank was leading the two horses out of the corral. Big Bay was saddled. Old Ben had his pack ready to be loaded.

She swallowed hard as an empty ache filled her. She would miss the quiet peacefulness of this place. The long shadows and cool breeze. The way the air smelled of pine and sage with a hint of dust.

But most of all she would miss this man.

"Get a hold of yourself," she muttered under her breath as she hurried into the cabin to finish packing.

"We'll eat on the trail," he said as he followed her into the cabin. He took his gun belt off the wall peg and belted it around his waist.

Once it was situated the way he wanted, he pulled the gun and spun the cylinder to inspect the cartridges. When he was satisfied, he reached up to pull down both his rifle and the shotgun. The man was going loaded for bear.

He really was in a hurry to leave, she realized.

She nodded, unable to speak. If she said anything words might come out that she could not take back. No, she told herself. She would not let him know how she felt. She refused to add that burden to him. He had already done so much for her.

As he packed Old Ben, she hurried around the cabin to gather up her things. There really wasn't much, she realized. Two weeks and she had left no mark on his world. Even the flowers in the canning jar sitting in the center of the table would die and be cast aside.

She wondered if he would think of her when he threw them out. And if so, what would he think? Probably he'd just be relieved to be rid of her.

When she was done, she spun to check one last time then gathered up yesterday's biscuits into an old flour sack and stepped outside. Her foot ached, but it was manageable. She handed Hank her carpetbag and he added it to the mule's pack.

Old Ben nudged her. Amelia laughed as she removed one of the biscuits from the sack to feed him. The mule really was a sweet dear. Hank talked of him being cankerous. But really, the mule was just a big baby.

"You're going to ruin him," Hank said with a scoff as he tightened a rope on the pack and tied it in place.

Amelia just laughed. At least someone should enjoy this day. Even if it was a mule. As she turned to give one of the biscuits to Big Bay a noise in the distance drew her attention. There, walking out of the trees, two men approached.

Her heart jumped as she gasped.

Hank frowned as he followed her gaze then froze when he saw the men. Every nerve told her to run. It was obviously Simmons' men. A tall thin man dressed in solid black, and a shorter, man with a red beard. She could see it in their eyes, the two men who had wanted to take her back to Simmons and some awful crib.

Her stomach tightened with fear as she remembered being drug through the alley to her doom. A sickness rose to her throat as she saw they had guns drawn, ready to take her back to Simmons. A sense of fear and failure filled her. Everything they had done had been for nothing. She was going to be taken back. Of that, there was no doubt.

"Stay here," Hank cursed at her as he stepped out in front of her and the horses.

"That's close enough," he yelled to the men approaching. The short bearded one laughed as he continued walking towards them. "Rusty wants her back and it looks like you don't have a say."

When he waved his gun back and forth, Amelia swallowed hard. Hank was helpless. Even he couldn't survive being shot. And at this range, they couldn't miss.

"Just give her back and we'll leave you alone," the tall one said as he looked left and right as if expecting to be attacked from the trees. All the while keeping his gun trained on Hank.

"No, we won't," Shorty said as he rubbed his jaw and let his eyes roam over her. "We want your gold also. Then we're going to have some fun," he added with a bone-chilling glare at her. "Rusty can take it out of my pay."

Amelia's heart pounded in her chest as she gripped the bag of biscuits. Could she get to the pack and the scattergun in time? Or would they shoot her? And if so. Might Hank get hurt in the crossfire? She swallowed hard as her feet refused to move. So many things could go wrong. And being taken might not be the worse.

No. Hank being killed would be the worse. She would never be able to live with herself if she caused him pain.

Hank stood there like a small mountain, blocking the men from her. She couldn't let him

145

get hurt. Not because of her. She stepped out from behind him to the side, being sure enough that if they shot at her, Hank would not be hit. "Don't shoot. I will go with you."

Hank spun on her with a look of pure mean on his face. "I told you," he yelled. "Stay ..."

But instead of finishing his curse, his hand dropped, and as if by magic, his gun appeared in his hand. He twisted and fired from the hip.

Amelia froze in place as the gun's explosion rocketed through the canyon. Another shot rang out. One of the horses screamed. Hank stepped in front of her, legs wide, shoulder's straight, a shield against the world's dangers, calmly pulled back the hammer and shot again.

Another shot was fired from the other men and a bullet whizzed by her head. Everything was so fast. One moment they had been packing the animals. The next, Hank was fighting to save their lives.

She peeked around his wide back to see Shorty face down on the ground. The tall man was holding his arm as he tried to back up into the trees. The gun in his hand shook as he tried desperately to steady his aim. The tall cowboy shot again but the bullet ricocheted off the woodpile a dozen feet away.

Hank started marching towards him with a fierce glare. As he marched, he lifted his pistol and took careful aim. When he fired, the tall man fell to his knees.

146

The cowboy frowned as he tried to work out what had gone wrong. They had the drop on the man. Their guns were out, his was holstered. Yet they had lost. It wasn't right, his expression said. It wasn't fair.

Amelia was frozen in place as her heart raced while she watched Hank cautiously approach the men on the ground. He used his boot to gently kick at them.

"Are they dead?" she asked.

"Pretty much," he grunted as he kicked at the black-clad man while pointing his gun down at him. "About as dead as you can get."

She sighed with relief as she fought to steady her shaking hands. Hank was alive. That was all that mattered. The both of them turned back to the cabin. Amelia gasped as her heart exploded in pain.

There, in the middle of the yard was Old Ben down in the dirt. The mule had been shot and died almost instantly.

Hank cursed under his breath, "I liked that mule."

Amelia's insides shuddered as she started to cry. Everything was wrong everything was all her fault. Hank had almost died because of her. Old Ben had been killed because of her. Two men lay dead because of her.

It was all too much. All she could do was stand there and let the tears fall.

The pain and anguish that filled her felt as if it would be with her always. But then Hank pulled her into his arms and gently held her.

"It will be all right," he whispered as he softly rubbed her back. Over and over, he quietly repeated the words. "it will be all right. I promise."

And somehow, she knew it would. Somehow, deep inside, she just knew that Hank would make her world all right.

Then she thought about him taking her over the mountains to be rid of her and once again the tears erupted as she once again started to cry into his massive chest.

It would never be all right, she realized. Her life would be empty without this man and there was nothing she could do about that fact.

Chapter Fifteen

Hank tapped down the second grave and stepped back. He'd chosen a place back in the pines. A place that could be forgotten. He wouldn't even put up a marker. These two didn't deserve one, not to his way of thinking. They'd come to take Amy. If he had his way, he'd bring 'em back so he could kill them again just on general principle.

His stomach turned over when he thought about what had almost happened. They'd gotten the drop on him. Pure and clear. All he could remember was the rage inside of him at the thought of her being taken. Nothing had mattered but saving her.

When the shooting started, all he could think about was killing them before they hurt her. That old familiar calmness had settled over him. A slow red haze. Jack used to say it was like walking into a cave. Everything narrowed down to just the enemy.

When that last cowboy had finally fallen, only then had he been able to take in the rest of the world and the fact that Amy was all right. Even now he shuddered thinking how close he had come to losing her.

Of course, once he got her over the mountain, he'd lose her for good. But that would be different he told himself. She'd be safe. Away from men like this. No longer in need of his protection.

The thought sent a cold shiver down his back. She'd no longer need him.

Grumbling to himself, he snatched the shovel and pick and started back to the cabin. Before burying the men, he'd skinned out Old Ben, stretched out the hide behind the shed. Amy didn't need to see the mule lying there in the dirt.

Amy had surprised him by being more upset about Old Ben than the men he'd killed. She'd taken that as a perfectly acceptable occurrence. But an innocent mule was unacceptable.

Again, one more reason she was remarkable.

The meat had been quartered but he couldn't see Amy agreeing to eat Old Ben. It wasn't in her. No, she'd been sweet on the old cuss. Maybe that Indian boy, he thought. Most Indians liked horse and liked mule even more. He'd have to figure out a way to get word to the boy.

As he stepped out of the pines into the yard, he pulled up short. There was Sonomma, the very Indian boy in question, with his bow and arrows in his hand. As if he'd seen an opportunity. More than one in fact. As he stood there talking with Amy like they were long lost friends.

Hank's hackles sprang up as he slammed to a halt.

Amy glanced at him and smiled weakly. She wasn't over the killing of Ben, he could see. That lost look in her eyes ate at his soul.

"Sonomma came to check on us," she said. "Isn't that sweet."

Hank grunted. The boy had come to check on her. But he decided not to make an issue of it. Instead, he hung the shovel and pick-ax on the cabin's wall then turned to face the boy.

The two of them stood there for a long moment. The boy didn't give away much. Hank had to give him that. A man couldn't read what he was thinking.

"You want the meat?" Hank asked as he gestured to the four quarters hanging by the larder.

The boy frowned as he looked for the trap. Why would this white man offer perfectly good meat?

"It is bad luck to eat your own mule?" Hank told him. Maybe the boy could accept that. "I'll trade you. The mule for a deer next month."

The boy's eyes grew wide as he looked at all of that meat, then slowly he smiled and nodded.

"I don't want your people traipsing through here," Hank told him. "You'll have to make several trips up over the ridge."

Again, the boy nodded as he hefted a hind quarter onto his shoulder. Hank's eyebrows rose. The boy was stronger than he looked. He started back towards the creek and the distant ridge when he stopped and turned back.

"The mountain grows angry," he said. "You take from her."

Hank snorted. "You let me worry about that. Ain't no mountain got me, yet."

The boy only stared then shook his head. "You, I don't care. But the woman should not go into the mountain. The yellow rock is not worth her life."

A cold chill ran down Hank's back.

Amy frowned as she looked at the boy then back at Hank. "Um …, gentleman. Need I remind you that neither of you are allowed to tell me what to do."

The Indian scoffed at Hank. "I was right, she is not your woman."

The two of them continued to stare at each other until finally the boy turned and disappeared into the trees. Hank could only shake his head.

"What were you two talking about?" he snapped at Amy before he could stop himself.

She frowned at him. "We were discussing Paris fashions," she said sarcastically.

He grunted as he shook his head. The woman was too fast for him. Always with the lip.

"What do you think we were talking about? His family. The school he went to. Things," she said with a cross look. As if she was disappointed in him. "You're not one of those men who look down on the Indians are you?"

Hank snorted. "Ain't none tougher. And when it comes to this land. None smarter. No, they may look at some things different, but that don't mean they're wrong. Just from a different world. And I know for sure that our world ain't got things figured out."

She frowned at him. "Then, why don't you like him? I see how you look at him. Like you think he's going to take something from you."

Hank snorted as he nodded to the cabin. "Can you get me some soap?"

When she stepped back out to hand him the bar of soap and a flour sack, he looked down into her eyes and said, "I don't like the way he looks at you."

Amy gasped and put her hands on her hips. "Hank Richards. Not everyone is evil. He's a boy."

Hank scoffed as he shook his head and turned for the creek. The woman was clueless. He couldn't explain it. And he couldn't exactly blame the young man. She was a pretty woman. Of course, the boy would look at her that way. But that didn't mean he had to like it.

When he got down to the creek, he removed his clothes, placed his gun belt close to hand, and walked into the pool. The cold water made him wince, but it felt good to wash away the dirt and Old Ben's blood. To let it all roll away down the stream.

What was he going to do? he wondered. He needed to get her away. Yet a part of him hated the idea. Things had changed.

She didn't flinch when he drew near. She didn't look at him like he was a monster. At least not most of the time. He would miss her laugh, he realized as the thought tore into his gut.

No, it had to be this way.

"Hank," a soft voice called from the trail.

"What?" he barked as he moved to his gun.

"Everything is fine," she assured him from inside the trees. See, he thought. That was what he meant by how things had changed. She could tell from the tenor of his voice what he was thinking.

"I brought you fresh clothes," she said. "If you leave your old ones by the creek, I will wash them. You'll need an extra set for the trail. Um ... if we're still going?"

He heard the hesitation in her voice. She was probably terrified about having to walk up and over those mountains. Or worse. Terrified of being stuck with him any longer than necessary.

"We'll leave tomorrow," he said as he stared up into the trees to try and find her. "You can ride Big Bay. He's used to carrying me, which means he can carry three of you.

Between him and me carrying a pack, we can bring along enough."

There was a long pause then she said, "All right," as she stepped out from the trees and held up his folded clothes. Her face grew pink as she glanced over at him then quickly looked away. "I'll leave these here," she said as she put them down on the very boulder that had trapped her foot.

He realized that the water was only to his waist and he should sink down but for some reason, he held still and watched as she glanced at him again. Their eyes locked and he felt his heart melt just a little. There was something in her eyes that called to him. Some unspoken thought that tugged at him.

"I'll wash the clothes," he said. "After all, I'm going to have to get used to taking care of myself again."

She swallowed hard, looked at him strangely for a moment, then lifted the hem of her dress and ran back up the trail.

It took every bit of self-control not to run after her. Instead, he pushed down the need inside of him and stepped out to dry off. No. she was going to leave and he needed to accept that fact.

That evening, as they ate a venison roast, greens from along the creek, and fried beans, an awkward silence fell over them. It was as if a heavy mist filled the room. A mist that stopped them from talking about what they wanted to say.

Instead, it was cautious looks and heavy sighs.

Hank grumbled in the back of his throat at the feeling of nervous energy mixed in with the awkwardness. See, he thought. This was the problem, things always got prickly. Unsaid thoughts and unspoken comments filled the air. That was why he didn't get along with people. They just naturally made things awkward.

It was like walking in one of them glass shops with pretty bowls and little figurines. He always felt out of place and uncomfortable. The wrong move and everything would shatter. A guy his size just naturally hated those kind of places. And this was worse.

"Thank you for dinner," he told her as he pushed back from the table. "I'm going to go check on Big Bay. He's probably missing Old Ben."

Her face fell at the mention of the mule and for a moment he thought she might cry. But instead, she squared her shoulders as she nodded and took his plate.

"It's been a long day," he said as he hesitated at the door. "We should probably call it a night. It's going to be an even longer day tomorrow."

"No cribbage?" she asked with a disappointed frown.

"Not tonight, But I'll pack the board for the trail."

She gave him a strange look then turned back to washing up after dinner.

Hank shook off a heavy feeling of guilt. It was wrong for him to want her to stay. The woman had a life in front of her. And that life didn't include being hidden away up in the High Sierra at a slow-paying gold mine.

There was nothing for her here. No women friends. None of the finer things a woman wanted in her life. Besides. She'd have to put up with him, and heaven knew that was nothing more than a woman's worse nightmare.

A grouchy miner. What more could a woman want?

When he left to go check on Big Bay, he noticed that all the mule meat was gone. The boy worked fast. He had to give him that.

"Bet he's basking in the praise of his people," Hank said to the horse as he started to brush him down.

The horse looked over at him, obviously upset that he was talking about a village of Indians enjoying his best friend for dinner.

Hank clenched his jaw and decided to just shut up. It only went to prove his point. He didn't even know enough not to upset his own horse.

As he brushed, a cold wind ran across his shoulders making him shiver. He cursed under his breath at the reminder that he needed to get Amy across to the other side. The wind put him in a disagreeable mood. Or at least, more disagreeable than normal.

He could only grumble and mutter to himself until Amy had enough time to get into bed. Then taking a deep breath he returned to the cabin.

She lay on her side, her face bathed in the soft yellow lamplight. Their eyes locked for a moment until she turned over to give him privacy to get ready for bed.

As he lay there underneath her, he listened to her steady breathing and tried to work out what that last look had meant. Was she upset at him for some reason? Or was it something else? He was still trying to understand when the darkness of sleep overcame him.

The next morning, he woke with a start. Something was wrong. Without moving, his ears stretched out trying to identify the threat.

The light under the door told him that it was early dawn. The creek gurgled but seemed suppressed. Then the realization that there were no bird songs hit him like a punch to the gut from a man who knew what he was doing.

He jumped from the bed to race across the cabin floor.

"What is it?" Amy asked as she sat up in her bed, her blanket held to her throat.

Hank didn't answer as he threw open the door.

There it was, the evidence that proved he was an idiot. That he had waited too long. Three inches of puffy white snow. And if there was three inches here. There was six feet up in the pass.

Chapter Sixteen

Amy couldn't wait to find out what was happening. What had scared Hank. His body language, the way he stood at the door just looking. It was worrying. Hank wasn't frightened of anything. But this had frozen him in place.

She quickly scrambled down the ladder from her top bunk then pulled a blanket off the bed to wrap around her shoulders. The morning was cooler than normal. Besides. She was never allowing Hank to see her in her nightclothes.

When she got to him, she gently rested a hand on his back to let him know she was there then looked outside and smiled.

Snow. It covered everything in a clean blanket. Hiding every blemish. Tamping down the sounds of the forest as if they were in a magical world. Snow was so rare in the Ozarks. She loved seeing it like this.

When she glanced up at Hank though, her stomach dropped. "What?" she asked. "What is wrong?"

He took a deep breath. "The pass will be closed."

She gasped with surprise. It was only a few inches. Really. This would close the pass to them? Then it hit her. They would not be leaving. At least not yet. A sudden thrill of happiness filled her, so much that she couldn't stop the smile on her face.

He frowned. "We'll have to wait until we get three or four days of thaw. We can follow the railroad to get over the flooded creeks and rivers. But the higher parts will be full until we get a good thaw. So, we are stuck here."

"How long will we have to wait?" she asked him as she fought to not appear happy about the prospect. He wouldn't understand and would think her a silly woman. She looked up at him waiting for an answer. How much more time would she have with him?

After a long moment, he shrugged his shoulders. "Weeks, probably. This is earlier than normal. So, we should get one more good warm spell before things close down for good."

Weeks. What a wonderful word, she thought. And maybe, if they were lucky. Weeks could drag into months.

"I'll stake out Big Bay," he said. "While you get breakfast ready. Then I'll head up to the shaft."

Amy frowned for a moment. He was really upset about something. Even more than normal. It was as if her staying a little longer was the worst thing possible.

"One good thing," he said as he pulled on his boots. "This will keep Simmons' men in their bunkhouses. No way they going out in this to hunt us."

Her stomach clenched into a tight ball at the mention of her enemies. "Won't they become suspicious when those two don't come back."

Hank shrugged his shoulders then stood up as he grabbed his jacket and rifle. "I bet they didn't report back they had found us. Just come in here expecting to leave with the prize and return as heroes."

She could only nod, it sounded correct. Those two didn't have the sense of tadpoles.

"So," Hank continued, "we should be fine for a few weeks. More than enough time to get you over that mountain."

All she could do was smile and nod as if that was her wish as well. The man was determined to be rid of her.

Later that morning, Amelia stepped outside to look up at the shaft on the mountain. The cold air nipped at her neck making her shiver. The heavy clank of a hammer striking a drill bit tumbled down the snow-laden hillside. She could easily imagine him, deep in the shaft, swinging that heavy hammer over and over.

The man was relentless. One day risking his life to protect her. The next, toiling away at back-breaking labor. Always trying to make things better. Her heart ached thinking about him.

She would take him his lunch. He would complain and admonish her for coming into the shaft. But tough. He would have to get over it. She had to do something for him. Some small effort to show how much she appreciated all he did.

Stew, she thought as she hurried inside the cabin to start a hearty meal. Plus, fresh bread. Exactly what a man would need on a cold day like this. Two hours later she started up the trail to the shaft. She'd placed the large bowl of stew and a warm loaf of bread in the bottom of a bucket.

The snow in the sunlight was melting, making the footing slippery. Her heart lurched when she thought of the coming thaw.

No. she told herself. She wouldn't think of that. Not yet. It was weeks away. Instead, she put her head down and continued up to the shaft.

When she reached the portal she was surprised to feel the warm air washing over her. It seemed the mine stayed the same temperature regardless of what happened outside. That meant he'd be working without his shirt, she realized and smiled to herself.

As she worked her way in towards the distant yellow light, she held her breath for a moment. The mountain of rock above her reminding her of just how close she was to death at any second. The thought sent a shudder through her body but she pushed it aside and carried on.

"Hank," she called between hammer strikes. The last thing she wanted to do was surprise him at the wrong moment.

He picked up the lamp and held it out to guide her to him. "I thought we agreed you wouldn't come in here," he said.

She froze for a second as she examined his exquisite form then pulled herself together long enough to scoff. "You dictated, but I never agreed. But if you want. I'll leave and take this stew with me."

He smiled and indicated a rocky outcrop for her to sit down. "Like I said, you're too smart for your own good. You know my weak spot."

Amelia laughed. Her heart raced with happiness. He hadn't sent her away. He hadn't dismissed her as if he didn't want her there. "A man your size needs a lot of fuel. It wasn't hard figuring that out."

He shot her a quick smile then sat down on the shaft floor next to her and tore off a hunk of bread to dip into the stew.

Amelia sighed with contentment when he gave her an approving nod. He liked her cooking. He always had. This was nice, she thought. The two of them sitting in the soft yellow light. Alone. The rest of the world forgotten.

"How is it going?" she asked as she pointed to the rock face.

He shrugged as he dipped his spoon into the stew. "About the same. Enough to make a living. Not enough to become rich."

Her brow furrowed. "Why don't you hire other miners to help. Couldn't you process more that way?"

The quick nod told her that he'd thought about it. "I could process more, but the wages would eat up anything extra we made. I'd just end up in the same spot but I'd have all the problems associated with working with other miners."

A heavy frown creased her forehead. "Are miners really that much of a problem?"

Hank laughed, almost choking on a piece of venison. "They're worse than a bunch of grandmothers. Each thinks they know best and anyone who disagrees is an idiot."

She could only nod. Oh, how she loved sitting here with him talking about his work. It made her feel slightly connected to him. As if he actually trusted her.

"No," he continued., "I've thought about it. If we hit a heavy pocket of gold and it looks like it will pay for a while. Then yeah. I'd hire some help. Set up a stamp mill to crush the ore. I'd have to put in a wagon road. A longer sluice, a bunkhouse, pack in a ton more supplies. Put in a race for the mill."

"I see, it does sound like a lot of extra work."

165

He snorted and nodded as he scraped the bottom of the bowl with the last piece of bread. "Yeah, but it's a good problem to have. It means we got too much money."

She smiled at him. "What would you do if you became rich?"

He frowned and looked off into the distance. "Settle down, I guess. Some house high up on a hill where I could look down on everyone else. You know. Every man's dream."

She studied him for a moment. "No wife, no children?"

He paused for a moment. As if some hidden thought was trying to get out. But then he shrugged his shoulders and tried to pretend he'd never thought about the subject.

"What about you?" he asked as he put the bowl and spoon back into the bucket. "What would you do if you were rich?"

Amelia smiled and shook her head. "That will never happen. People like me don't become rich."

"I'm serious," he said as he laid back against the shaft wall and frowned at her. "What would you do?"

She took a deep breath and sighed. "A nice house, in a nice town with friends around."

"No husband, children?" he asked with a strange look. The darkness and weak yellow light made it hard to read him. Even harder than normal.

Suddenly, her insides froze solid. This conversation had become too personal.

He didn't smile at her as they both became very aware of each other. Amelia felt her heart melt as she looked into his eyes. This was the man she wished for. The man that should be hers.

The two of them continued to stare into each other's eyes when a distant rumble poked around the outskirts of her awareness. She had dismissed it until she saw his eyes open wide with fear.

"Blast," Hank yelled as he grabbed her and threw her to the ground covering her with his body. Amelia was about to protest when she felt the ground underneath her back shift, first one way then the other. Her heart jumped into her throat. An earthquake.

"Hang on," Hank yelled as he forced her into a curled up fetal position so he could cover more of her while the ground continued to shake.

Within seconds. A new noise filled the shaft. A cracking snapping sound that sent a bolt of pure terror to her soul.

She felt him tense up around her as the ceiling twenty feet away let go. The ground stopped shifting long enough to bounce them inches off the ground as a heavy shower of dust and small rocks washed over them. Her ears popped as the lamp flickered out.

Darkness.

A darkness she had never known before. A new night filled with dust that made her cough. The ground finished rumbling as the last of the rocks fell around them.

Hank grunted as he rolled off of her. She could hear rocks shift and tumble off him. He had protected her once again.

"Are you all right?" she asked into the darkness as her heart raced with panic.

"Yes," he grumbled but she could tell he was lying.

She held her breath as she frantically tried to think of what to do. Her heart pounded with fear as she tried to peer through the blackness. Nothing, it was impossible. Then, it hit her with a sickening realization. There was no distant light from the shaft's opening.

Suddenly, a match flashed and she winced away from the bright light. Hank held the match to the lamp and brought it up to the pile of fallen rocks. The glass chimney lay in shards in the dirt.

It was as if someone had opened a zipper and let loose the mountain itself. Rocks and gravel were stacked up all the way to the top of the shaft, blocking any escape. She bit back a scream at the realization they were trapped and would probably die in this very spot.

Chapter Seventeen

Hank examined the cave in. His insides tightened up as he saw just how bad it was. The shaft had let go along the seam. There was no telling how far it went. It could go back all the way to the opening portal in which case they would never get out.

They'd die in here. His insides turned over at the thought of Amy dying like that. The air would give out, and they'd twist themselves into knots gasping their last breath like fish tossed onto the bank of the river.

An anger began to build inside of him. How stupid could he have been? Letting her come in here. All because she brought him food and he enjoyed her company. He had put his own happiness ahead of her safety.

He held his breath as he lifted the lamp and trailed the bare flame along the top edge of the cave in. His focus narrowed in on the small yellow flame. Praying it would dance and show some indication of airflow.

Nothing.

The lamp's flame was as immovable as the rock surrounding him.

He sighed heavily. They were in trouble. They were on their own. There weren't a dozen miners fighting to get into them. And the air wouldn't last long.

"Is there anything I can do?" Amy asked him.

"Hold this," he said as he passed her the lamp. Her eyes were as big as moons as she looked up at him. He saw it in her face. She knew how much danger they were in. She was a smart girl.

There was only one way, he thought as he started pulling out boulders, scraping away gravel to get at more boulders.

Once the first easy ones were free, he had to use his hammer. The large rocks were interlocked, tied together like a giant puzzle. Years of work had built him for this moment. Every muscle strained to get them through.

As he swung his hammer against stone, he felt his lungs having to work harder. The air was already failing them.

His insides refused to let anything happen to her. He would die fighting to get her out. Nothing was more important.

As he pulled another rock from the pile. Sonomma's words echoed him his head. The Yellow rock was not worth her life. Truer words had never been said, he realized. Nothing was worth more than Amy.

He continued to work, cursing and grumbling. The temperature in the small enclave became warmer as the air became thicker and thicker. He had to shake his head to clear the fuzziness as the sweat poured into his eyes.

Please, he begged as he pulled another rock away.

But no sooner had he removed one rock than another fell from the ceiling into its place.

"No," he cursed as he frantically fought to get them out.

"Hank," Amy said from behind him as he struggled against a particularly tough stone.

"What?" he snapped without turning back.

"I need to tell you something," she said with a hesitant voice. "Before we die. I need you to know something."

"We're not going to die," he cursed as the stone finally came free.

He heard her sigh heavily behind him and knew that she was worried. She must be terrified but the woman didn't cry, didn't complain. She was as solid as the rocks he was fighting against.

"I need..." she began. "I need you to know that I am in love with you. If we die. I wanted you to know that."

He froze for a moment as the words sank in. "Amy that's nice and all," he said as he returned to pulling out rocks. "And I figure I feel the same way about you. But right now, I got bigger problems."

"Hank," she gasped. "Really? You love me?"

He snorted and stopped so that he could turn and look back at her. "I've been in love with you since the first time you back talked me. But really Amy we don't have time for this right now."

Her brow furrowed as she reached up and pulled at him. "I refuse to die without kissing you one time."

Sighing heavily, he stepped down from the pile of rocks.

His world shifted as their lips came together. It was like coming home for the first time in his life. Like finding the one place in this world where he belonged. A need and lust-filled him. Along with a tender caring that surprised him.

This woman meant everything to him and always would. There was no doubt in his mind.

He forced himself to pull back and stare down at her. "You could make a man forget he's trapped under a mountain of stone."

She smiled up at him and his insides collapsed. He loved her so much.

"Get us out of here," she said as she held up the lamp. "We have a life to live and I refuse to miss it."

He laughed as he shook his head and attacked the rock pile. What a woman. The kind of woman who could birth a nation of warriors. The kind that would make a man happy to be alive.

Once again, he started pulling at the rocks. Using his hammer against the worst of them. At other times, he used an iron drill bit to pry out trapped stones. Pushing and pulling them free and letting them tumbled down the pile to the shaft floor.

His muscles ached, his head swam, yet he pushed himself. He had to get her out. There was no other option. Clenching his teeth, he fought like he had never fought before.

Amy stood behind him holding up the lamp. Shifting to give him the best look with each different rock. Was the flame smaller? Was the air turning bad that fast?

He took a deep breath of stale air and focused on moving forward. On forcing a way through the pile of stone.

He had created a path almost three feet deep when he realized the rocks were no longer coming down from the ceiling to replace the ones he'd removed. Yes, he thought with a burst of hope and a surge of new energy. Maybe he could get through.

He had to crawl up into the small tunnel, grab a huge stone then wrestle it out of the hole. The darkness inside the escape tunnel made it hard. The rocks tore and ripped him each time he slid out of the hole.

"I need more light," he called back to her, his voice echoing like a man in a well.

173

There was no response, his heart lurched as he scrambled back out of the small tunnel to find Amy sitting on the floor, the lamp in her hand. She was looking off into the distance. Her chest heaving as she fought to get air.

His insides turned to jelly with pure fear. He had never known such fear. Even in the Army. Nothing had hit him like this. He couldn't fail her.

Yet, he could feel his muscles refusing to work as they cried for air. A sharp pain bore into his shoulders yelling at him to just stop and lay down next to Amy.

"No," he cursed under his breath as he crawled back up the slope and into the small tunnel. His bare arms scraped against the rock, ripping long tears into his skin and muscle but he pushed it aside as he focused on getting through.

His fingers began to bleed but he pulled at the next boulder, determined to get it out of the way. But the evil stone refused to budge. The escape shaft was too small to swing a hammer. The boulder too big to pull. He'd have to dig out another foot of stone to the side to get it out.

There was no time, he realized as his mind wandered. No time.

Forward, a voice deep inside whispered to him. If you can't pull maybe you could push. Gasping for breath, he anchored his legs and began to push.

174

At first, there was nothing. He was literally pushing against a stone wall. They were going to die. If they didn't get air, they would be found a hundred years from now by some old prospector.

Sucking in the last of the air, he pushed again and felt just the slightest movement. Just enough.

"NOOOOW!" he screamed as he put every ounce of his remaining energy into the stone. Her life depended on it.

A slight popping sound echoed through the mine then the stone shifted. An inch at first, then it let go and tumbled down the far slope. A rush of dusty air brushed past him.

He let his head drop to the stone beneath him as he lay there, sucking in glorious air. That elixir of life.

"Hank," Amy called weakly from behind him.

"I'm through," he told her as he scooted backwards out of the hole. "I can see the portal opening on the far end. We're going to make it."

She smiled up at him. "I never doubted that we wouldn't. There is too much beast in you to ever fail."

He flinched at her words until he saw the smile on her face as she reached up to touch his arm.

"I love that part about you. It makes a girl feel safe knowing you are there to save her."

His insides tightened up as he accepted his fate. He was in love with Miss Amy Dunn and his life was never going to be the same.

.oOo.

Amelia's heart melted as she looked up at her hero. No other man could have gotten them out. Then the realization sank in of what she had told him and what he had said back to her. That he loved her also.

Were his words a way to keep her calm? Nothing more than the words of a man who thought they might die and he hadn't wanted to make her feel worse?

Was that it?

"Um ..." she began. "About earlier ..."

His brow furrowed as his eyes flashed with anger. He sighed and pointed to the small tunnel he had built.

"Hurry up," he said. "Now is not the time. I swear you'd talk until the mountain washed away."

She smiled to herself. There was the Hank she knew so well.

"Help me up," she told him as she started to climb the cave in. The small tunnel frightened her until she saw the distant white light of the shaft opening. Freedom.

Using her knees and elbows she began to enter the escape tunnel when she felt her hips become stuck. How had Hank gotten through here?

"I'm stuck," she yelled back at him.

"Here," he said as he placed a hand on her bottom and pushed.

"Hank," she gasped, as her cheeks grew warm at his liberties.

"Amy," he said and she knew he was shaking his head at her. "We are trapped under a mountain. And I've seen you naked. Oh, and by the way. You said you loved me. That gives me permission. Now scoot."

He pushed again and she felt herself break free. Her heart soared as she climbed out the far end and crawled down the outside of the cave in. He had acknowledged what she had said and he hadn't sounded upset. Not even dismissive. Surely that meant something.

Within seconds he poked through the tunnel and handed her the lamp. She quickly put it aside so she could offer him a hand. His shoulders and fingers were bleeding. His body was covered in dirt and sweat. Yet no man had ever been more handsome.

"Can we talk now?" she asked as her heart raced. She desperately needed to know if he had meant what he had said minutes before. Did he really love her? How was that possible? She had been nothing but a hindrance.

"No," he said as he took her elbow. "Not until I've got you out in the sunshine where you belong."

She sighed internally as she reached down to retrieve the lamp. As she took the handle, the large rock next to her flashed a bright reflective light. She froze as she moved the lamp closer.

"Hank?" she said as she studied the boulder. Solid quartz the size of a large bucket. It must have been the stone he had pushed out of the tunnel. And here it was flashing at her. "Is that gold?" she asked.

A three-inch wide seam a foot long of what looked like pure gold was attached to the rock. It extended along the entire top of the rock.

Hank grunted as he wiped his hands on his trousers then turned to inspect what she was looking at. She heard his breath hitch for a second. Then he let out a long slow whistle. Without saying anything, he took the lamp from her hand and crawled back up the pile of rock behind them to inspect the ceiling and the empty space above the cave in.

Amelia held her breath as he worked. The tension was intolerable. "Is that gold?" she asked again. "It would be more than you've collected so far. All in one rock."

He pulled back out of the tunnel and looked down at her. His face had a strange look. Surprise mixed with something else.

"It would be the biggest single find I ever came across," he said. "If it weren't for what I just saw above us."

Her stomach clenched up tight. Was he telling her the truth?

"Looks like you're going to get your house on a hill," he told her as he scooted down to take her elbow. "The first thing a rich lady needs to learn is that she doesn't belong in mine shafts. They have a habit of letting go."

Chapter Eighteen

Air. Sweet, glorious, outside air. It tasted of life, Amelia thought as she stared up at the crystal blue sky.

Life, everything was so delicious. The trees had never seemed so green. The snow so white. Even the rocks under her feet made the world feel solid.

Hank stood next to her. His eyes closed as he drew in deep breaths of the clean air. A tall, strong mountain of a man who had once again saved her. And he said he loved her. Could it be true? Could she believe him? Did he even know what it was to love someone?

Surely, in all of history, no one had ever felt about another human the way she felt about him. She watched him closely, taking in his three-day-old beard. The dust and blood. The large shoulders and relaxing brow.

She took a deep breath of contentment until his eyes suddenly sprang open.

"What?" she asked as she held her breath.

He shook his head with a deep frown. "I forgot the bucket and your stew pot."

Amelia could only stare up at him then laughed. A hard, happy laugh. The man was so silly.

"You also forgot your shirt," she said. "Really, what am I going to do with you." Then smiling at him she took his arm and said "Come on. Let's get you cleaned up and dressed more properly. A rich man shouldn't be walking around without a shirt. It is unbecoming."

He laughed and started down the trail after her.

When they got inside, she pointed to a chair and said, "Sit."

"I should get washed up."

"Sit," she said again, more forcibly this time as she retrieved Consuela's salve. She placed the medicine and a bucket of water on the table. Tore a flour sack then started washing away the dirt and blood.

As she ran the wet cloth down his strong arms, she bit down on the inside of her cheek to stop from saying or doing the wrong thing.

He watched her, his eyes following her every move. She focused on her task. If she looked into his eyes she felt as if she might melt.

When she finished, he laughed softly.

"What?" she demanded.

"You're pretty when you blush," he said.

Her cheeks grew even warmer and she knew her face was beet red.

"Of course," he continued, "you're beautiful all the time. So that's not hard."

Amelia had to close her eyes and try to slow her racing heart. When she was somewhat in control of herself once more. She opened her eyes to find him looking at her intensely.

"I've got to tell you something, Amy," he said as he stared into her eyes.

She sighed. "I like it when you call me Amy."

He chuckled. "I got to tell you that I'm glad we said that stuff in the tunnel before we found the gold."

She felt her brow furrow in confusion. "Why?"

He laughed again. "This way I know you didn't marry me for my money."

Her jaw dropped. Marriage. He was talking about marriage. "You want to marry me someday?"

He suddenly frowned. "Not someday. Tomorrow if I had my way. We could go to Reno. They got a judge there or, if you want a church wedding, we could do it that way. I'm pretty sure the place won't burst into flames if I walk through the door. But if it does. We'll buy them another one."

Amy studied him for a moment he was serious, she realized. Then a sudden thought pounded into her brain at the word Reno.

"What about Simmons?"

His smile dropped. "I'll deal with him."

The confident tone sent a shiver down her back as a sense of foreboding filled her. Rusty

Simmons would have a dozen armed men. Each one a killer. They wouldn't let Hank get within a dozen feet of the man.

"What about somewhere else?" she asked hesitantly. "Or maybe, later. We could wait."

He frowned at her. "You don't want to marry me do you?"

Her heart broke. "No, no. That's not it. I just don't want you fighting Rusty Simmons and his men."

His frown grew even deeper. "So. Now you don't think I can protect you? Is that it?"

A feeling of pure panic filled her. He was misunderstanding everything.

"Listen. I understand," he continued, "I probably didn't read things right."

The panic feeling tore into her stomach. She reached out to hold his head in place so she could stare into his eyes. "You listen to me, Hank Richards. I am in love with you. I want to marry you. But I don't want you getting killed. Not until we have half a dozen grandkids."

He laughed then took a deep breath. "We'll leave in the morning. We'll stop by Dusty and Jack's. Then I will go and talk to Simmons."

She frowned as her stomach turned over. A sense of doom filled her. There were so close. But he couldn't take on the whole world. Not and survive.

"Don't worry," he told her. "I can be very persuasive."

She shook her head. "This isn't some rock you can split with your hammer and a drill. These are mean men with guns."

Cocking his head to one side he smiled. "Amy. You ain't seen mean until you see me upset. And if Rusty Simmons ain't willing to change, then I'll just have to teach him different."

"Couldn't we just leave?"

He snorted. "We've got a rich mine. I ain't leaving it. Not only that, but once people find out how rich it is we're going to have people trying to take it away. One thing I learned over the years. The only thing harder than finding gold is holding onto it once you got it."

She sighed heavily. She'd never change his mind.

"I won't let you go in there alone," she said as she stared into his eyes to let him know just how serious she was.

He scoffed and waved his hand dismissively. "That's not happening."

The two of them stared at each other in a battle of wills. Finally, she slumped in defeat. But deep down. She knew she was only delaying the inevitable. No, she wouldn't let him fight alone. This was her man and nothing could be more important than helping him.

"We'll talk about it later," she said.

He sighed and shook his head, but had the good sense to let the matter drop. The fool probably thinks he will win, she thought.

"How far is it to your friends?" she asked as she gathered up the medicines and water bucket.

"About a day. We'll leave in the morning, get there tomorrow afternoon."

Her heart jumped at the thought of meeting his friends. Would they like her? She had no one. No person in this world that she wanted him to meet. The thought sent a sadness through her. Oh, how she wished her father had lived to know Hank. He would have been impressed.

As she took down a shirt for him her eyes glanced at his broad shoulders and she smiled to herself. Every woman at home would have been jealous. The thought filled her with pure glee at imagining the looks of surprise and envy she would have received if she and Hank were to return there.

It was the kind of thought that could make a woman happy to be alive. That and the thought of sharing her life with this man.

As he buttoned his shirt, he glanced over at the bunks then back at her. A strange look in his eyes made her insides tighten up with anticipation and a little fear. But the exciting kind of fear that made her want to laugh.

"I'll sleep up in the mine shaft tonight," he said as he let out a long breath.

"What? Why?" she asked as a new fear washed through her. The thought of him inside that death trap filled her with a new terror.

He sighed heavily then stared at her. "The truth?"

She bit her lip as she nodded.

"I don't know that I can keep my hands to myself. You're too tempting."

Her insides melted with pure happiness. It was the best problem any woman ever had. The man she loved wanted her. They would be married. Need they wait?

"It's important that we wait," he said with a heavy sigh.

"Why?" she asked as her cheeks grew warm. But she didn't look away.

He sighed heavily. "I want it legal. Recorded. If something happens. I don't want you ..."

Simmons, she realized. If Hank was killed. He didn't want her being left as a fallen woman or with an illegitimate child. The man was such an idiot. She stepped up next to him. Close, almost touching and looked up at him as she placed a hand on his chest.

She held her breath as she stared into his eyes. "I don't want to go through life having never been with you."

There, it was out. The truth. Her heart raced. She had declared her deepest feeling.

He grimaced and shook his head. "I want that more than I have ever wanted anything," he said with a deep frown. "I know that I am going to regret this. But we can't. Not until we are married. Something inside of me. It'd be like tempting fate. Giving me what I want most in this world just so it could be taken away."

Her stomach clenched until she fully understood. He was right. It would be like tempting fate. They had just escaped from a horrible death. They had become rich. Discovered their love with each other. It was all too much too soon.

He was terrified that if they pushed things too far too fast. They would lose everything. She sighed heavily as she came to accept his decision.

"But you are not sleeping in the mine," she told him with her hands on her hips, determined.

He smiled then nodded. "Fine, but you take that crutch with you to bed to fend me off if'n I change my mind.

She relaxed and nodded. It was only a few days. She could do anything for a few days. Although deep down she knew this would be the hardest thing she had ever done in her life.

Chapter Nineteen

Amy watched as Hank studied the tracks in the dusty road then glanced back at her.

"Jack and Jenny live up that way," he said as he nodded up the western fork in the trail towards deeper into the mountains. "The prettiest little valley you've ever seen. This creek comes down from their place."

Amy swallowed hard then nodded as she fought to hide her nervousness. She wanted to meet his friends but so much depended on their impression. What if they didn't like her? Would they try to talk Hank out of marrying her? Would he follow their advice?

The thought sent a bolt of fear straight to her heart. She loved him so much. Yet, she didn't really know him. Not this aspect of him. Friends. It was hard to think of him having friends. And he'd been through so much with them. The war. Years of shared pains and triumphs.

"We're in luck," he said after he finished examined the wagon tracks. "I think Jenny and Jack are at the C-Bar with Dusty and Rebecca. They like to get together every so often."

Amy took a deep breath and tried to give him a pleased smile. But she knew it didn't reach her eyes.

Hank's brow furrowed for a moment then he smiled. "Don't worry. They're going to love you."

"What if they don't?" she asked as a sinking feeling filled her.

He laughed and shook his head. "Then I'll get new friends."

Now it was her time to laugh. "You get new friends? Let us be honest. That is unlikely."

His face lit up with a big smile. He was so different when he smiled instead of scowled. Her heart turned over with love.

"Come on," he said as he started up the northern fork. He had walked the entire way. She'd offered to switch out with him but he'd simply looked at her as if she was talking nonsense.

"Thank God they got a bunkhouse," he said over his shoulder. "You can stay in the main house and I'll bed down in the bunkhouse. I ain't going through a night like last night ever again."

Her cheeks grew warm with embarrassment. It always did when he talked like that. She knew what he meant though. Last night had been long and intense. She had lain there listening to him breathing beneath her. Waiting for him to leave his bed and come to her. A hope and a fear mixed into some strange new emotion she had never experienced before.

She had spent the night hoping to hear his soft snore. It would let her know he had fallen asleep. And therefore, she could relax. But the man had tossed and turned throughout the night until finally, the birds let her know that they had made it through the night.

He was right though. Never again.

"Tell me about your friends?" she asked as they continued on.

He shrugged. "Knew Jack and Dusty in the war. We got in more scrapes than most. Jack married Jenny, it's a long story and I'll let them tell you. But you'll like it. You women enjoy those romantic stories."

She smiled. The man was more observant than she realized sometimes.

"Rebecca is a little different. Rich, from back east. Dusty was a bit of a saddle tramp who spent too much time at the poker tables if you ask me. Ended up saving her ranch. Again, one of those romantic stories."

Amy smiled to herself. No one would ever be able to top her story. Of that, she had no doubt.

"Rich? you said. How rich?"

He glanced back at her and smiled. "Don't worry. She ain't one of them high toned women. At least not anymore. This country will beat that out of a person. No, Rebecca is nice. How she ever puts up with Dusty I will never know. But she's got him walking the line. Never would have thought it."

"And Jenny?" she asked.

He smiled softly. "Jenny is like the sister I never had. Sweeter than apple pie and yet with a spine of forged iron. You and her will get along. You're both alike in that way."

Her heart melted at his compliment. What made it even more special was the fact the man wasn't even aware of how much impact his words had on her. He'd simply spoken the truth as he saw it.

Taking a deep breath, she tried to calm her happy heart unless it run away with itself. Instead, she looked out over the country surrounding them. It had changed from the mine. No snow. More sagebrush and fewer trees. Dryer, hotter. The High Desert, Hank called it.

Heavy gray clouds threatened from the far horizon, the mountains rose up to the west.

She missed their mine up in those mountains.

"Have you thought what you're going to call your mine?" she asked. "I mean don't famous mines have names."

He smiled at her. "Ain't mine, it's ours. How about Amy's Hope."

She blushed but shook her head. "No, it needs to be something that captures its essence."

"What do you mean by essence? Sounds like an awful big word for a hole in the ground," he asked with a frown.

"The feel. The country. Something like ... Sweetwater Ridge. You know. The mountains, the creek. The gentle nature of the area."

He frowned for a moment as he continued to walk. "Don't know that any gold mine was ever considered gentle like. Just ain't their nature. But if that's what you want. That's what we'll call it."

Her insides relaxed. She had just named a rich gold mine. He hadn't pushed back or dismissed her as silly. He'd simply accepted her desires. She knew full well that it would not always be like this. He would be stubborn and obstinate. But, here, now, he was being sweet.

Who would ever have thought that a man like Hank Richards could be sweet? It seemed to disprove everything she had ever thought she knew.

"Besides," he said with a sly smile. "Every time I use that name. It will bring up pictures in my mind of you laid out down by the creek. You know the one I'm talking about.

"Hank!" she said as she leaned down to slap him on the arm.

He laughed, "Yes, Sweetwater Ridge. It has a good sound to it."

Her cheeks grew warm. The man was a tease and a pest and she loved him for it.

As they continued on she thought back over her life. The hardscrabble upbringing in Arkansas. The way her father had been treated.

Her mother dying when she was young. The failed crops and angry neighbors.

The horror that had been Rusty Simmons and her trip west. All of it washed over her as she realized that it had all been worth it if it led her to this man. This time. Every hurt, every disappointment was being offset by what she had found.

No sooner had the thought occurred, than a sense of doom filled her. It could all be taken away so easily. As if someone had held out a treasure, then snatched it away when she reached for it.

The nervousness inside of her could not be contained. Something was going to happen to ruin everything. It always did. Why should this be any different?

She looked down at the man she loved and grimaced at the thought of losing him. Yet she knew that it would always be like this. He would insist on tackling danger head-on. He would crawl into pits in the ground searching for wealth and treasure. He would face down anyone who tried to stop him.

It was the kind of man he was, she realized with a sense of acceptance. It could be no other way. It was one of the many reasons she loved him. Yet it put him in danger. Risked their future happiness. The twin nature of the situation tore at her. He was a beast. A hard man who faced the world. The kind of man who would never back down. The kind of man who took risks.

Yet, would she want him any other way? What would she prefer? Hank working in a bank or behind a merchant's counter?

No, she thought with a shudder. The man would shrivel up and die in such a world. The part of him she loved the most would disappear. No, she would have to accept the fact that he would be putting himself in danger on a daily basis. It was who he was and she would have to learn how to live with it if she was to have him.

"Here we are," Hank said as he led them up over a small hill and around a corner into a courtyard. Amelia examined her new surroundings. The main ranch house to the right. A barn and bunkhouse to the left. Her heart began to race with anticipation as she gathered herself for battle.

"Uncle Hank," a young boy said as he raced across the dusty courtyard to throw himself at the big man.

"Henry," Hank said as he picked the boy up and swung him around before tossing him into the air.

The boy, probably no more than five or six, squealed with laughter as Hank caught him then pulled him into a deep hug. Amelia smiled as her heart melted. She would never have believed that the monster she had known could be so gentle with children.

"This is Henry Tanner," Hank said to her. "My godchild, namesake, and the toughest roughest little man this side of the Pacific Ocean."

The little boy beamed as he wrapped his arms around Hanks's neck and shot her a quizzical look. Hank put him down and said, "You go tell your momma and Miss Rebecca we're here."

The boy nodded, gave her a last look, then shot off to the main house.

Hank watched him for a second then took Big Bay's reins and led her to the corral. "They grow up so fast," he said as he reached up and lifted her off the horse.

"Hank, I can get down by myself," she said as her heart jumped at his touch. He lifted her so easily. Once more showing the difference between them. He was so male. So … manly.

Once she was down, she quickly smoothed her dress and made ready to meet his friends. He laughed as he leaned down to whisper to her. "You enjoyed it as much as I did."

Her cheeks flushed with heat just as two women stepped out of the main house, followed closely by two tall cowboys. The blond woman carried a small baby on her hip. The brunette turned back to hand her own baby to the man behind her. The father, Amelia assumed.

Amelia stood a little straighter as she took a deep breath.

"Hank Richards," the blond woman said as she looked from him to Amelia, obviously very curious as to why her friend had brought a strange woman to them. "It is about time you showed up. I was going to send Jack up into those mountains to dig you out and get you back here to civilization. At least for long enough to stop you turning into a hibernating bear."

Then she surprised Amelia by reaching up and pulling him down so that she could kiss Hank on the cheek and give him a hearty one-armed hug while still holding the baby. She cared about him, Amelia realized. Really cared about his well-being. The thought made her like this woman immediately.

Before Amelia could completely take it all in, the pretty brunette stepped forward and held out her hand to her. "Welcome," she said. "I'm Rebecca. I thought I should introduce myself. If we waited for Hank to carry out social conventions we'd be waiting until next summer."

Amelia smiled to herself. The woman had teased Hank. Always a good thing as long as it was done in fun. The man was too perfect as it was. He needed to be kept in his place.

Hank coughed as he scrambled to regain control and to dismiss the subtle jab from Rebecca. "Jenny, Rebecca," he began. "This is Amelia Dunn, from Arkansas. And we're getting married. Thought you might want to know."

Both women blanched, then their eyes lit up with happiness as they stepped forward to congratulate her.

Immediately, the world became a swirl of names and stories. Jack and Jenny and their three children Henry and Hanna and the little baby Amy.

"That's what Hank calls me," Amelia said to the baby as she squirmed in her mother's arms.

Then it was Dusty and Rebecca Rhodes and their baby son John. The owners of the C-Bar ranch. Amelia swallowed hard as she fought to take it all in. This was not what she had expected. People who knew and cared for each other. It was so different than home, and an entirely different world than a hidden mine up in the High Sierra.

The two cowboys both tipped their hats to her. Dusty examined his friend with a deep frown and shook his head. "Only you could go into the mountains looking for gold and come out with a pretty woman."

Before she could register Hank's reaction, Rebecca slipped her arm into Amelia's and started to lead her to the main house. "You have to explain everything. How ever, did you convince Hank to ask you to marry him."

Amelia smiled as she went with her. "Actually, he never really asked. He just insisted."

Both Rebecca and Jenny laughed. "That sounds like our Hank. But why ever did you agree?"

She took a deep breath and shrugged. "After the third or fourth time, he saved my life. I just thought it was the smart thing to do. Besides. You know him. He could sweet talk the birds out of the trees. He has such a way with words."

Jenny coughed with surprise until she realized that Amelia was teasing.

"Oh, you are going to fit in just fine," Jenny said. Amelia could tell that the woman was almost relieved as if she had been worried that Hank's new wife would make things difficult. It surprised Amelia to realize these people were worried about her as much as she had worried about them.

It spoke of how important Hank was to them. The thought sent a warm feeling of happiness through her.

"So, tell us everything," Rebecca said as she led her into the house. "How did you meet?"

Amelia's stomach clenched up as she looked over her shoulder at the three men standing in the courtyard. What should she tell these women? Would Hank be upset at her if she mentioned Rusty Simmons and what had almost happened to her?

"Don't worry about them," Rebecca said kindly. "They'll stay out there talking about horses and cows. Unimportant things compared to true romance.

Amelia smiled at her. Yes, she would tell them what really happened. She could trust them they would not judge her.

But deep inside, she still felt that sense of doom. One more thing had gone right. His friends were nice. When would things change? When would they start going bad again?

Chapter Twenty

Hank took a deep breath as he looked at his two friends. "I'm going to kill Rusty Simmons and I don't want either of you getting involved."

Neither so much as blinked. Jack pursed his lips and shrugged his shoulders. "You don't get to decide what we do or do not do."

Hank ground his teeth. He had been afraid of this. "You've got families to think about. They are more important. I won't be the reason those kids grow up without a father."

Both Jack and Dusty frowned as they pondered his words. He knew these men well. They were like brothers. Closer in some ways. They would go through the gates of Hades for him. It was his responsibility to make sure that didn't happen.

"Why?" Dusty asked. "I mean, Rusty Simmons is lower than dirt. But he runs a nice saloon. Why'd you want to kill him?"

Hank took a deep breath then explained what Simmons and his men had done. Tricking Amy and trying to force her to work in his brothel. Both of them sucked in a quick breath. Abusing a good woman was beyond the pale. A man could get away with a lot. But that was unacceptable.

"Then he sent men in after me. Tried to get her back. They killed my mule."

Neither asked what had happened, they knew him. They knew that neither man still lived.

"I figure he won't stop. So, I thought I'd go in and take him out before he gets me."

Jack shook his head at him. "You can't just go in and kill a man. They got laws now. The country is getting civilized."

Hank frowned. "It'd be a fair fight. Guns or fists. Then I'd kill him."

Dusty laughed and shook his head as he slapped him on the back. "You need to think this through. The man has a dozen gunmen working for him. He ain't going to let it be fair. After all, no man with any brains is going to get into a fair fight with you. They'd lose every time."

"I don't care," Hank grumbled. "I won't have Amy worried about him coming after her. I can't watch her all the time and work a gold mine. He started this by sending them two in after us. I aim to finish it now."

Jack studied him for a moment then shook his head. "You love that woman, don't you?"

Hank smiled slightly. "More than is possible. She doesn't think I'm some monster."

"Then why do you want to make her a widow before you even get married?"

"You've got to think, big man," Dusty said. "It's different when there is someone to leave behind. You got to take them into account. You can't just go in like a bull charging in the suttler's store. Breaking everything in sight and letting someone else clean it up."

A wave of worry washed through Hank when he thought about Amy being left alone. She'd have the mine. But she'd be scammed out of it by some slick banker. And there'd be no one between her and the worst of the world.

"I can't walk away," he said. "I'd be looking over my shoulder for the rest of my life. Simmons ain't the kind of man who takes to losing what he thinks is his."

Jack sighed and said, "We'll all go in. The three families. The women won't be kept away from a wedding even if we tried. Dusty and I will talk to Simmons. Maybe we can make him see to walking away and letting the feud die off."

"We can be convincing," Dusty said with a smile.

Hank felt his back tense up. "I won't have you two fighting my fights for me."

Jack laughed. "Why not? You done it for us enough times. Besides, there won't be no fighting. Not if we do it right."

Hank studied him. The man had always known what to do. As their Sergeant in the Army, he'd led them out of danger more times than Hank could count. He had a natural understanding of how to make things happen.

Where Hank had a habit of going in swinging and figuring out what to do after the fight was already over. Jack was different. He could think three and four moves ahead.

"All right," Hank said with a heavy sigh. "We'll do it your way. Amy was ready to chew my ear off if I went in without her. At least this way she can't be mad at me."

Dusty smiled and shook his head. "I never thought I'd see the day Hank Richards worried about what a slip of a girl thought, one way or the other."

Hank shot him a quick frown. If he was criticizing Amy he and his friend would have a long, hard discussion that would probably end up with someone punching someone.

Dusty quickly held up his hands. "I ain't criticizing. I'm saying you've already learned the important part of being a husband. It took me three months before I figured it out. Don't tell them their opinion don't matter. That you're going to do it anyway. It makes 'em crazy."

Jack nodded. "And I imagine Amy is even tougher. She'd have to be to take you on. Can't imagine a harder job for a woman if you ask me.

Hank laughed. He had been so lucky to have these men as friends. It had taken a war to break through his barriers. But these men had never failed him.

.oOo.

Amelia sighed when she finished telling her story. She let them know everything. From the shunning in Arkansas to Simmons and his intentions. Dressing like a boy so that Hank could sneak her out of town and up to his mine. The men coming after them. Hank killing them. Even Sonomma, the Indian boy.

Of course, she kept back the part about being trapped naked down by the creek and Hank helping her. Some things they didn't need to know.

She told them about the cave in but held off about the high-grade gold they'd found. That was Hank's choice as to who to tell.

"Remarkable," Jenny said as she leaned forward and placed her hand on Amelia's knee in reassurance. "No wonder you fell in love with him."

Amelia frowned and shook her head. "It wasn't because he was saving me all the time. It was more than that. Oh, don't get me wrong. A big strong man saving your life can turn a woman's head. Of that, there is no doubt. No it was more."

Both of the other women raised an eyebrow, silently asking for more information.

Amelia smiled as she remembered. "It was the way he played cribbage. He didn't get mad when he lost. That surprised me. He was so intense all the time. Determined to defeat anything that got in his way. But with me. It was like he didn't look at me as something that needed to be defeated. Do you understand?"

Rebecca smiled slyly. "Of course. Also, wide shoulders don't hurt."

Amelia blushed and quickly looked down so they would not see just how much those wide shoulders and the rest of that large hard body had impacted her.

"There were other things," she continued. "Tender moments that surprised me. I mean just look at him. You'd think he wouldn't have a sweet bone in him. But that's not true. He can be very sweet when he wants to."

Both Rebecca and Jenny smiled as they nodded. "It can be hard to see," Jenny said. "Most women don't take the time to look for it."

Amelia shrugged. "Being hold up in a cabin with the man for weeks I got to see a part of him he doesn't show to the rest of the world."

Rebecca was about to say something when the front door opened and all three men walked in.

"I sent young Tom up to your place," Dusty said to Jenny. "To care for your stock until you return."

Jenny frowned as she shot her husband a questioning look.

"Dusty has invited us to spend the night," Jack said. "That way we can all go into town together tomorrow."

Now it was Rebecca's turn to shoot her husband a questioning look.

"That's where most people have weddings," Dusty said. "We thought you two might wish to attend."

Both Jenny and Rebecca cried out in pleasure as Amelia looked at Hank. The big man appeared worried. Was it about them getting married? Or was it something else?

"What about Simmons?" she asked him as she held her breath.

"That man needs to be run out of town," Rebecca said with a curse.

"No," Amy gasped. "I won't have Hank fighting him."

Hank shrugged, then pointed to his friends. "These two have convinced me to let them handle the issue. They say they will just talk to him and convince him to mend his ways."

"Hey," Dusty said. "That's the role of best man after all. Smoothing out problems."

"And I will walk you down the aisle," Jack told her with a smile. "If that is acceptable."

"A church wedding," Jenny said with glee. "It is about time one of us had a regular wedding."

Rebecca smiled. "Judge Benson will be disappointed. He hates losing business to Reverend Sawyers." Then she turned to Amelia. "You are going to need a wedding dress. Come with me."

Amelia felt herself being led away, but she looked over her shoulder at Hank, desperate to know that he really wanted this. His smile smoothed the worry in her heart. Not completely, but enough.

The next few minutes were a whirl of activity as Rebecca examined dress after dress in her armoire until she stopped for a moment. then pulled out a cream colored silk dress that made Amelia's heart stop. White lace and alabaster buttons.

"I couldn't," she said as she shook her head. The dress was too beautiful. Too rich for someone like her.

Rebecca laughed. "I will never have reason to wear it. It was the latest fashion a few years ago. A Paris design. And then I came here and it seemed such a waste until now."

Amelia hesitated as she gently reached out and ran her fingers over the sleek fabric. What would the people at home think if they saw her walking down the aisle in such a dress? To marry a man like Hank.

Their eyes would drop out of their heads.

"Besides," Rebecca said as she placed a hand on her stomach. "I will soon be so big it won't fit. Please, let me do this. Consider it a wedding gift."

Amelia took a deep breath then nodded. She wanted Hank to see her in this dress. She could imagine him staring at her with need. The kind of look from the man a woman loved that made her feel good about herself.

"Gloves and a hat will finish it off perfectly," Rebecca said as she pulled down a round box from the top shelf.

"And a little gauze. A veil," Jenny said as she removed another dress with a gauzy wrap around the collar. It amazed her, these two women acted as if they were sisters, sharing and teasing. Suddenly, a desperate hope filled her that they would come to accept her in the same way.

The feeling of emotion was so strong that a tear threatened the corner of her eye.

"Thank you," she said as she sniffed to try and hold the tear from falling. "You have both been so sweet to me."

Jenny laughed. "It's we who owe you. If you hadn't come along, Rebecca and I were going to have to scour half the state to find a woman who deserved Hank. After all. There is nothing more challenging that an eligible bachelor. It upsets the balance of the universe."

All three of them laughed at the truth behind the words.

Rebecca suddenly gasped. "A bath. You won't have time tomorrow. But tonight? After dinner, before you go to bed. You will have a sit-down bath. Consuela has a system down of heating buckets of hot water. We have a bathtub in the house, just off your room."

Amelia froze as she thought about the wonderfulness of being covered in warm water. Clean and fresh for her wedding. The idea was overwhelming and she could no longer hold back the tears.

Both Rebecca and Jenny smiled sympathetically as they pulled her into a welcoming hug.

Later that night as she leaned back in the tub and soaked in the warm water she sighed heavily. Life did not get any better. It was as if a lifetime of tension and worry were pulled out of her body.

The soft scent of lavender and rose petals in the soap was an especially nice touch. It made her aware of the softer things in life. She had a lot to learn from a woman like Rebecca. A woman who appreciated what was important.

And with Hank's new wealth. She too could live like this. The thought seemed amazing. Her, poor Miss Amelia Dunn, was to become a wealthy married woman. Impossible.

There was also so much to learn from Jenny. She had watched as the blond woman had interacted with her children. Treating each of them special in their own way. But it was the secret look she shot her husband that told Amelia so much. She appreciated and loved him.

Yes, there was so much she needed to know.

During the dinner around the big table, the group had talked and teased like the old friends they were. Something Amelia had never known. That easy comradeship of people who knew what could be said. Shared experiences and values.

She'd learned of the fight between Jack and the original owners of the C-Bar. Of how her future husband and Dusty had stood with him against his enemy.

Then she had learned of how Dusty had saved this very ranch against rustlers and an evil banker.

They talked of the war, but always in careful easy terms. Only remembering the good times. She knew they were saving the women from the worst aspects. But she could feel it there underneath. The shared pain and loss.

And of course, they talked of the range, the price of beef, the weather, even state politics. All things that could impact them directly.

Amelia had let the information flow over her. She had been desperate to ask questions about Hank but realized that they were things he needed to share on his own. The last thing she had wanted was to upset him the night before his wedding.

Her wedding, she thought as her stomach clenched up with worry. What would Simmons do? Could Dusty and Jack really talk him away from taking action? It seemed farfetched in her view. The man was pure evil.

No. She knew in the pit of her soul that things would go wrong. They couldn't go well. Nothing in her life had ever gone well. Why should this be any different? Especially since she wanted it so much.

A sense of pending doom hovered over her. She knew she shouldn't succumb to the feeling. But it could not be ignored. Something bad was going to happen. Something that would stop her from obtaining the happiness she had always wanted.

Chapter Twenty-One

Hank rode Big Bay at the rear of the group. Amy sat in the buckboard with Rebecca and Dusty. Little John on her lap. It felt strange to be separated from her, he thought with a shake of his head. Jack and Jenny and their passel of kids were in front in their wagon. Upon their return, they would peel off and head for their home.

But for now, they were all going to town to stand with him and Amy at their wedding.

The thought made him snort with disbelief. Him, getting married. The thought seemed preposterous. And to a woman like Amy. It was impossible. He was the monster. Women didn't look at him as marriage material.

Yet, Amy had never judged him like that. She had worked under his skin until the thought of life without her seemed wrong. An affront to the way the world should work.

He took a deep breath and tried to pull his thoughts away from the woman. She'd have him wandering around in a cloud of silly love if he wasn't careful. He had a mine to build. Riches to capture. If he was going to give her the life she deserved, then he must make sure he did it right.

There was the entire build-out aspects of things. Men to hire. Equipment to buy. Most of all he needed to protect it all. Once people found out what he had discovered, some would try to take it from him.

More claims, he thought to himself. He needed to lay claim to the ridge across from the shaft. That vein might very well cross both ridges. He'd need to lay claim to other sections, parallel to his claim. There might be more veins hidden from view. Sections of rock folded in on itself.

Then there was the whole paperwork aspect of things he thought with a shudder. He'd need someone to do the books. Keep track of things.

It's your wedding day, he told himself. Those things could wait until tomorrow. Today, he needed to focus on Amy and keeping her safe.

Jack and Dusty would talk to Simmons. It was best this way. If he tried to talk to the man, he'd end up killing him.

A slow smile crossed his face as he thought about putting his hands around the man's neck and squeezing until the light left his eyes. Of course, the sheriff and judges would get involved and ruin a perfectly good wedding day. No, it was better that Jack and Dusty handled it.

He glanced forward to find Amy looking over her shoulder at him. She smiled quickly and her cheeks flushed pink. His insides melted. The woman tore at his soul with a simple look. He was going to have to be careful or she'd be running things. Then he laughed to himself. Who was he kidding? He'd do whatever it took to make her happy. That was why he had been put on this earth.

Rebecca said something to her and they both fell into conversation. Hank took a deep breath and tried to return to thinking about the mine, but of course, he failed miserably.

When they reached the outskirts of town, he nudged Big Bay forward to take the lead. If Simmons knew they were coming in, he might take action before any of them were ready. Besides, he wanted to see the look in their eyes when they saw him. It would tell him all he needed to know.

As they passed the Red Grove two lounging cowboys stood up. Their eyes opened wide in surprise. One turned to rush into the saloon. The other shot Hank an evil glare. Then his stare shifted off to examine his friends. When they saw Amy, the man eyes narrowed in concentration then opened wide again as the realization sank in.

Hank stared him down, silently begging him to make a move. The cowboy swallowed hard but he didn't back down. Instead, he simply watched as the group passed. Hank wondered if they knew he had killed their comrades?

Swinging down off Big Bay, he tied him to the hitching post outside the Sutler's then reached to hand down Amelia. Her pale, frightened face tore a hole in his gut. The thought of her being frightened bothered him down to the bottom of his soul.

"It will be all right," he assured her.

She smiled up at him then pulled him down so that she could kiss him on the cheek.

Hank felt his cheeks grow warm. People were watching. His friends were smiling at him. It was enough to make a man want to go back up into his mountains.

"Come on," Rebecca said slipping an arm into Amy's and pulling her towards the store. "We have so much to get ready."

Hank's stomach tightened at the thought of Amy being out of his sight.

"You two going to talk to Simmons?" he said to Dusty and Jack after the women and children had entered the store.

"After the wedding," Jack said. "It will change the conversation. Simmons knows no miner or cowboy is going to put up with a wife being troubled with. There are too few of them. He'd have a riot on his hands."

"That's the kind of thing that leads to vigilantes and long drops with short ropes," Dusty added.

Hank shook his head. He didn't like it. There were too many holes. Too many ways for things to go wrong.

Dusty studied him for a moment then shook his head. "We need to clean you up. A new set of clothes. A shave might be nice. Women like that kind of thing."

Hank took a deep breath and nodded. "I need to get Charlie some clothes to replace what we took when we snuck Amy out of town." What he didn't tell them was that he needed to get into the Sutler's to make sure Amy was fine.

When he stepped into the store, Amy shot him a quick smile. She and the other women along with Mrs. Pruitt, the store owner's wife, were looking at bolts of fabric. He knew that they would use the backroom to get Amy ready for the ceremony.

"What can we take back to our cabin?" she asked him.

He froze. It wasn't right. Taking a woman up to that small, rough cabin. A woman like Amy deserved so much more.

"You get whatever you need. I'll purchase a couple of mules."

Her smile softened. She was worried, he realized. Something was bothering her.

"Are you sure about this?" he whispered as he pulled her away from the others so they could have some privacy.

She frowned for a moment. "Are you?" she asked.

He snorted. What a ridiculous question, then he saw the fear jump to her eyes and his insides tightened up. "A man don't often get a chance to hitch himself to a woman like you. He'd be an idiot for not marrying a girl like you, Amy."

216

She smiled softly. "And I know for a fact that you are not an idiot." She sighed, then looked up into his eyes. "And neither am I. Yes, I want this. More than I have ever wanted anything. But it is going so fast. I worry that you are making a mistake."

Hank's insides relaxed as soon as he realized she still loved him. Still wanted him for a husband.

"That's enough," Rebecca said as she stepped up next to them. "We have a lot to do. And you can't see her in her dress. Get what you need and disappear. Meet us at the church in ... an hour."

"Two hours," Jenny interjected.

Hank took a deep breath and nodded. It would mean leaving her. But only until they could get her to the church.

After he'd gotten what he needed he returned to Big Bay and pulled the shotgun to take with him. Dusty raised an eyebrow but had the good sense to keep quiet. Hank refused to walk through this town unless he was loaded for bear.

"I'm going to Charlie's," Hank said as he started for his friend's shack. The sooner they got this wedding over with the sooner they could deal with Simmons.

"I ain't letting you out of my sight," Dusty said. "You're likely to change your mind and skitter off into those mountains. Or make a wrong turn when you pass the Red Grove."

Hank ignored him as he walked down the middle of the street. If someone wanted to take a pot shot at him, the extra distance might make a difference.

As they passed the Red Grove saloon, the bat-wing doors swung open to let Rusty Simmons step out onto the boardwalk. The man was dressed in a frock coat with a starch white shirt and collar with a diamond stick pin. The man's flat brimmed black hat didn't hide the evil glint in his eyes.

Hank's stomach clenched up as he gripped his sawed-off shotgun.

"No, you don't big man," Dusty said as he grabbed his free arm. "You ain't making her a widow, remember?"

Hank locked eyes with his enemy and let him know that this was not over. Simmons nodded back to him, acknowledging the fact.

By the time they got to Charlie's, Hank pounded on the door while he pushed down the need to destroy. At least for now.

Charlie greeted them at the door with bleary eyes and a scrunched up frown. "Working nights at the Ophir mine, guarding their strong room," the cowboy said as he stepped back to let them in. "Someone hit the bank in Carson two weeks ago."

"I'm getting married and you're invited," Hank said as he handed over the folded clothes.

Charlie's eyes opened wide as he looked at Dusty to confirm this impossibility. Dusty smiled and nodded.

"Has she met him?" the man asked with disbelief.

"I'm cleaning up here," Hank grumbled as he ignored his friend's question. "You got a razor worth anything?"

"She has," Dusty said. "And wants to marry him anyway."

Charlie stared in disbelief as he retrieved his having gear. "Simmons was looking for you. She the reason why?"

"Get dressed," Hank said as his stomach clenched up. "And after the wedding, I want you to take over the security for my mine. I'll pay you twice what you're making now. I can't be everywhere at once."

Both Dusty and Charlie froze as they stared at him. Slowly Charlie broke into a large smile. "You hit something. Something worth guarding."

Hank finished buttoning his new shirt. "Let's just say I'm going to be ordering a stamp mill. I'll probably need to build a bunkhouse for a dozen men."

Charlie shook his head. "Don't let Simmons hear that. You wouldn't be the first to lose a rich mine to scum like him."

Hank snorted a quick laugh. "I could only be so lucky that he'd try. But Jack and Dusty are going to make him see sense."

Charlie glanced over at Dusty and raised an eyebrow. Dusty, however, was studying Hank with a quizzical glare.

"I know what you're thinking," Hank said to Dusty. "But she told me her feelings before I hit that pocket. She told me when she thought we were both going to die in that hole. So, get that silly idea out of your head."

Dusty nodded, accepting his friend's statement.

"Besides," Hank said as he belted his gun onto his hip. "I'd have married her anyway."

Chapter Twenty-Two

Amelia buttoned the last of the alabaster buttons and ran her hand down the silky fabric. It was impossible to believe she was wearing such a dress. Oh, how she wished her father could see her in it.

He should be the one walking her down the aisle instead of Jack. A sadness filled her. Life could be so unfair sometimes.

Rebecca gave her a quick smile of approval.

Jenny opened the door and poked her head in. "I'm going down to the church to make sure that preacher is ready. Jack will be out front if you need him. I'll be back in just a minute."

Both Amelia and Rebecca nodded. Jenny shot her a quick smile and a brief nod then disappeared.

"You know," Mrs. Sawyer said, "We have a veil that would work better than that gauze. A lady ordered it but never came to get it."

Rebecca pulled the laces of the dress tight and tied them off. "She probably decided not to marry. Either that or the man backed out. They have a habit of doing that."

"Not my Hank," Amelia gasped.

Rebecca smiled softly as she shook her head. "No, not Hank. He isn't that kind of man. Besides. He loves you too much. It'd take an army to keep him away from that church."

Amelia relaxed as she twisted to examine herself in the mirror.

"You want to come see this veil?" Mrs. Sawyer said to Rebecca. "And we got some fancy hatpins." Amelia nodded for her to go check it out. She trusted Rebecca's sense of fashion. Who wouldn't? The woman had a Paris designed dress. She knew what would work.

Amelia closed her eyes and took a deep calming breath. She was about to become Mrs. Amelia Richards. Married to a man that curled her toes.

She used those few quiet moments to think about their future. She had just reached the thought of children when she felt cold metal against her temple.

"Shush," a menacing voice whispered. "Or we will kill him slow."

Hank! They had Hank she realized as she spun around to find Simmons' man Bennet holding his gun pointed at her head. The other hand with a finger to his lip as he gestured to the back door.

At the door, the young cowboy Denning smiled, waiting for her.

"I swear," Bennet whisper. "You come with us now and we can work this all out. You give me any trouble and we will kill your man slow and hard."

Amelia's heart rose to her throat. They had Hank. All she could think about was how once again he was being put into jeopardy because of her. She didn't think of Simmons and what he would do to her. All she knew was that she had to go with these men.

She thought back to the story Jenny had told her. About how men had tricked her to trap Jack. Was that what was happening here?

It didn't matter, she realized. She couldn't take that risk. If they had Hank, she would have to give herself over to them.

Biting down the fear tearing at her stomach she lifted her chin and stepped out the back of the store. She needed to get to him. She needed to know that he was all right. When Denning grabbed her elbow, she pulled away and shot him her best glare.

"Keep your hands to yourself," she cursed.

The crazy cowboy balked and she could tell that he was fighting with himself. His fist clenched and her insides tightened as she prepared to be struck. But he pulled back and took a deep breath.

Turning, she followed Bennet as they made their way behind the buildings. She thought of running, darting out into the street and screaming for help. But they had Hank. And one thing she knew without a doubt. They would carry out their promise.

No, she had no choice. She took a deep breath and forced herself to continue on until they reached the alley she remembered so well. Please still be alive, she silently begged. All that mattered was that he was still alive. If she could get to him before they killed him. She could make a trade. Make Simmons understand that if he hurt Hank, he'd never have her cooperation.

It was the only thing she had to offer. Her cooperation.

Bennet opened the back door of the saloon and pushed her into the long hall. Once again, she was hit with the aroma of tobacco smoke and beer. His stomach turned over and she thought about pulling away but forced herself to continue forward. Bennet kept his hand on her back to stop her from running. What the man didn't understand was that she needed to go to Hank. She couldn't resist until she knew that Hank was all right.

When they entered the main room of the saloon, four cowboys at a far table stared at them. One gave Bennet a quick nod then pulled his gun from his holster and laid it on the table.

Two of Simmons' girls stood at the bar, leaning back, watching her. She could see the regret and sadness in their eyes. The younger redhead had a nasty bruise to the side of her face. Amelia's insides turned over. She would get no help from them. They knew this was wrong but they would do nothing to stop it. No one stood up to a man like their boss.

"Up here," Bennet said as he pointed to the stairs. "He's in the office."

Amelia studied him for a long moment, then lifted the hem of her fancy wedding dress and started up the stairs. Both Bennet and Denning followed closely.

When she got to the door, she didn't wait for Bennet to open it. She turned the knob and marched in.

Immediately, her stomach dropped. No Hank. It had been a lie. Behind a desk, Simmons studied her with his hands folded across his stomach. She took a deep breath to scream when Denning stuffed her mouth with a dirty bandanna, tying it tight. The rag tasted of dirt and sweat.

"In the chair," Simmons said to his men. Both of them grabbed her by an arm and forced her to sit in the chair as they unraveled ropes.

Simmons continued to stare at her. Studying her as if he were one of them professors looking at a bug trapped in a glass jar.

"Really, Miss Dunn," he said. "Your debt has grown significantly. You will be an old, used up woman before you pay it off."

Amelia pulled away from Denning's grip and reached up to pull the gag from her mouth. "Hank will kill you for this."

Simmons pursed his lips then nodded. "I expect he will try." Then he looked at his men. "Tie her to the chair. I don't want to have to listen to her while we wait."

225

Amelia's heart broke with guilt and shame. They were going to use her for bait to trap Hank. She had been such a fool. Jack had been close. If she had but screamed, Hank would have been safe. Now he would charge in and be killed.

She thought of the cowboy downstairs who had taken out his gun and rested it on the table in front of him. They were waiting for Hank, she realized with a sinking sickness. They would gun him down before he ever got to her.

A deep terror filled her. Hank would be killed and she would spend her life being used by men like Rusty Simmons.

Desperate to stop it, she pulled against the ropes holding her, but it was useless. She was tied up like a spring calf for branding.

This was it, she realized. The doom she had been anticipating. That feeling that had constantly crawled between her shoulder blades. The ruin of her dream. The worst of outcomes.

A sadness filled her as she thought of all that would not happen. She would never marry Hank. Never lie with him in their marriage bed. Never watch him hold their child. A tear threatened to fall but she pushed it back. She would never give Simmons the pleasure of seeing her cry.

Instead, she lowered her head and fought to figure out some way to stop it. Someway to keep Hank alive. Raising her head again she tried to talk around the gag. Weak mumbles were all she could produce.

Simmons glanced over at her then indicated Bennet should lower the gag.

"If you scream," the brothel owner said, "it won't change anything. But, I find it annoying and I punish people who annoy me. Just ask Alice downstairs."

Denning twittered with an ugly grin.

Amelia's stomach turned over with fear. Once her mouth was free, she worked her jaw and swallowed as she desperately tried to get the taste of the rag out of her mouth.

"You were saying?" Simmons asked as he leaned back in his chair.

Amelia took a deep breath. She had no choice. It was the hope to save Hank. "I will work for you. Do what you want. And I won't fight or run away." The thought made her cringe inside and sick to her stomach.

"But," she continued, "you need to leave Hank alone. If he is hurt. I will spend every day of my life fighting you."

Simmons studied her for a long moment then slowly smiled as he shook his head. "Do you really think I have gone through all of this because of you?"

She could only stare at him in confusion. What was he talking about?

"No," he continued, "that man took from me what was mine. I don't care if he'd taken you to China. I would track him down and kill him. Never forget that. You can never escape"

Her heart slammed to a stop. There was nothing she could do to stop this. Simmons hated Hank and would do anything to destroy him.

He watched her then sighed heavily. "The only reason you are here is because I want him to know that I have you before we kill him. I want him to know that he has failed." He hesitated slightly then sneered. "And the money I will make off of you, of course."

She could only stare in amazement at such evil. She had known it had existed, but to see it so blatantly displayed made her world view shift. When she glanced at Bennet, he simply shrugged his shoulders then pulled the curtain back to look out the window to the street below.

They were watching for Hank, she realized. Waiting to kill her man.

Once again, she pulled at the ropes, but it was hopeless. Hank would storm into the saloon and be shot immediately. She knew him. Nothing could keep him away. This was a man who took on mountains. Relentless. Determined. With a kind heart and a strong mind. But none of that mattered. He wouldn't think it through. He'd barge in and be gunned down before he got a dozen feet.

"Please," she begged Simmons. "Isn't there any humanity in you?"

The man frowned for a second, then shook his head. "No, I don't think there is."

Amelia slumped in her chair. Defeated. She had lost and Hank would pay for her failure.

Chapter Twenty-Three

Hank heard a sound outside and turned to face the door as it slammed open. Jack stood there with a heavy scowl. Hank's stomach dropped.

"They took her, Amelia," Jack said. "From the back room. I was out front. I didn't even know it had a back door."

The world turned red in Hank's mind as his stomach curled up into a tight ball. Everything fell away. They had Amelia. That was all that existed. He grabbed the shotgun from the table and started for the door.

Jack held up a hand to try and stop him. Hank pushed him aside like a fancy curtain and stormed out of Charlie's shack. He was going to kill Simmons and anyone who tried to stop him. He should have done it his way from the very beginning.

"Hank," Dusty called as he raced to catch up. "Stop, think it through."

"You know as well as I do that it is a trap," Jack said from the other side of him.

Hank bit down the angry words bursting inside of him to be free. This wasn't his friends' fault. It was his. All his.

"If you go in there like this," Dusty said as he put a hand on his shoulder. "They'll gun you down before you get through the door."

Hank shrugged it off as he turned down main street. The world had become focused as if every sense had come alive to its full potential. As he walked, he scanned for danger. Years of experience had taken over. He was going into battle. Threats and dangers needed to be identified so that they could be eliminated.

People on the street took one look at him and backed away. He could see it in their eyes. The monster was on the loose.

"Think," Jack said. "If you get killed. Amelia will be his. Do you want to do that to her?"

"Listen to your friends," Charlie said from behind him. The small cowboy had followed. Great, Hank thought, more people to worry about. If they'd just let him alone none of this would have happened.

Hank spun on his friends. "He's got her," he yelled through clenched teeth. "If he hurts her, I will literally skin him alive and make it last for days."

The three looked back at him as if they were looking at a crazy man which wasn't far off.

Jack sighed, "You can't do that if you're dead."

Hank started again, there was nothing they could say that would stop him.

"Let us go in first," Dusty said, "You come in from behind. Like we did that time at Coulter's Ferry. Remember."

Hank slammed to a stop as he studied his friend.

"You want to get that girl," Jack said, "then do it smart."

"They won't be expecting us," Dusty added as they both desperately tried to stop him from making a mistake. "They won't know what to do. We'll go in gentle, just two men wanting a beer. But we'll be in position when you come in."

Hank gritted his teeth. Every instinct told him to charge in there and start killing until he got her out.

"You can do what needs to be done," Jack said. "They are all yours. Just let us get in there ahead of time to keep them off your back."

Hank spit on the ground. "I told you. I don't want you two involved. I won't make Jenny and Rebecca widows. You too, Charlie, this ain't your fight."

Dusty shook his head. "Too late. Amelia is one of us. If you go in there and get killed. We still got to go in after you and get her."

The seriousness in his eyes startled Hank. They really did consider Amy as one of theirs. They would die to rescue her. The red rage parted just a little. Just enough for him to play out the scenario. All four of them killed and Amy still in Simmons' hands.

"I get to kill him?" he asked Jack.

His friend nodded.

Hank took a deep breath then growled. It wasn't fair. Every part of him demanded he charge in there. But they were right. After a long silent moment, he let out a long breath, then nodded. He would do it their way. Both Jack and Dusty sighed with relief. Charlie looked on as if he didn't believe him.

"Give us five minutes to get into place," Jack said, "then you come in from the back."

Hank nodded as he ground his teeth, desperate to get started. Every second they had her was time to be hurting her.

"Charlie," Jack continued, "you stay here with him to stop him jumping off too early. Then take up position outside the front to make sure no one comes in after we get started. I don't want any surprises."

The small cowboy nodded.

Hank stared up the street. "Your five minutes has already started."

Jack and Dusty nodded to each other then started up the street. Both men checked to make sure their guns rested easy in their holsters. Dusty glanced back, Hank sighed, his friend was obviously worried he'd change his mind and charge in there like a bear on a rampage.

Taking deep breaths, Hank forced himself to hold in place as he ran through a dozen different scenarios. One thing he'd learned early in the

Army was that no plan survived first contact with the enemy. Things changed, shifted. That was why he preferred to just go in there and kill anyone in his way and let God sort 'em out.

When he couldn't hold still any longer, he twisted and started down an alley between the newspaper building and the undertakers. He glanced at the business signs and wondered which would make more money off the next few minutes.

"It's not time yet," Charlie said as he hurried to catch up.

"It will be by the time I get to the back of the saloon," Hank cursed. He could feel Charlie rolling his eyes but he ignored him. Not one second extra. If Jack and Dusty weren't there then that was their problem. They'd miss out on all the fun.

"Well, try to be a little less obvious," Charlie said. "You stand out like a small mountain in the middle of a lake."

When they got to the back of the Red Grove, Hank cursed and pointed to the street. "You get into position. They'll be in there by now."

Charlie swallowed then nodded. "You be careful. I like the thought of that job. Double pay. A man could live high on the hog that way."

Hank snorted. It took every bit of control not to rush in there. But he gave Charlie time to get in front, then reached out and slowly turned the knob on the back door. He held his breath as he stepped into the long dark hall.

He immediately saw Jack and Dusty leaning on the bar. A beer in front of each of them. The rest of the room was off to the side out of view. How many? he wondered.

Jack glanced down the hall and saw him. Leave it to Jack, he'd put himself in the perfect position. Without giving anything away, his friend dropped his hand and rubbed his leg with four fingers.

Four of them. Hank thought with relief. This was doable.

He pulled up at the corner and looked at his friends. A redhead, one of Simmons girls, joined Dusty and ran a hand over his shoulder while giving him her best flirtatious smile.

His friend turned to examine the girl then, shook his head. "I'd be careful, Alice," he said "if my Rebecca finds you like this. She's likely to pull your hair out by the roots."

Alice blanched, shot him an angry look then turned away. The girl wasn't an idiot. But best of all, Dusty had gotten her out of the line of fire.

Hank took a deep breath as he prepared himself. Keep your head, he told himself as a calmness settled over him. It always did when he went into battle. The red rage was pulled back and replaced by a settled calmness. Kill or be killed, it was that simple. And make sure it happened to the other guy.

Jack gave him a quick look from the corner of his eye then turned and punched Dusty in the shoulder.

"That's it," he yelled. "You are as wrong as can be, I don't care what you say ..."

That was Hanks cue. He gripped his sawed-off shotgun and stepped into the room. In the corner, four cowboys were watching Jack and Dusty argue. They were arranged behind a round table, the four of them facing the front door.

Jack's diversion was all he needed. Three steps and he was there.

All four jumped to their feet. The skinny one in the end reached for the gun on the table. Hank swung the butt of the shotgun against the man's head. He fell like a sack of potatoes.

"I wouldn't," Dusty said. Hank looked over to see both of his friends with their guns drawn. Pointing at the four, now three cowboys, stopping them from going for their guns.

"Where is she?" Hank asked them.

They each looked at the others, silently telling them to stay quiet.

Hank's huge left fist slammed into the chin of the closest cowboy. A loud crack echoed through the room when his jaw shattered. He also fell to join his friend on the floor.

"I asked you a question," Hank said through gritted teeth as he poked the next man's gut with the shotgun.

The cowboy looked down and swallowed hard. He knew that the wrong move could end up with a six-inch hole in his gut and an eight-inch hole out his back.

"Simmons will kill you," the tall skinny one next to him said.

Hank frowned as he continued to hold the weapon on the first cowboy. He shifted and brought his knee up into the tall man's groin.

The man groaned as he curled up on himself.

Hank turned back to the final cowboy, the one pinned by his shotgun. "You going to tell me or am I going to have to take you apart bit by bit?"

The cowboy swallowed as he glanced over at Jack and Dusty.

"Don't be looken at them," Hank said. "I'm the one gets to kill you if I want."

The man's face drained of all color, then his shoulders slumped as he nodded up the stairs. "First door," he whispered.

Hank growled under his breath as he turned to rush to the stairs. At the bottom, he turned on the lone remaining cowboy. "If she's hurt. I'm coming back to hang you by your heals over a campfire."

The man stared back, perfectly aware that he was looking a long slow death in the eye.

"You two stay down here," Hank told his friends. "I don't want you getting in the way."

Both of them had the good sense to nod. They'd seen him in action before.

Chapter Twenty-Four

Amelia quietly worked at the ropes binding her wrists. She'd rubbed them raw but was no closer to getting free than when she started.

Bennet kept looking out the window. He stood to the side so no one could get an easy shot. She almost laughed to herself. Hank wouldn't stand off and take long shots at a figure in the window. He'd come in like a bull after a matador.

She knew her man. There was no doubt in her mind.

Gritting her teeth, she glanced over at Denning who stood in the corner. He'd be behind an opening door. A person rushing in wouldn't see him. Denning would have a perfect opportunity to shoot him in the back.

How could she warn Hank? He needed to know what he faced. She was sure he would plow through those men downstairs. But what if he were wounded? Regardless, the shots below would alert the men in this room. They would be ready for him.

Simmons was still sitting behind his desk running his fingers down a large green ledger. He'd removed his hat and coat and hung them on a hat stand behind his desk. He didn't wear a gun, but she had seen one in his top drawer when he had pulled out the ledger.

The man made her insides curdle like sour milk. The smarmy smirk that permanently rested on his face reminded her of all those people from home who had hated her father. Like they knew everything. As if they could never be wrong.

If she ever got her hands free, the first thing she was going to do was slap him just to get rid of that smirk.

The clock on Simmons' desk chimed two for the hour. Her heart fell. She was supposed to be walking down the aisle on Jack's arm. Hank was supposed to be standing next to the preacher. She wanted to see the look in his eyes when he saw her in this dress.

She wanted a life with the man she loved. That was all. She just wanted to be left alone to enjoy her life with Hank. Instead, she was trapped in a room with three men waiting to kill Hank.

A feeling came over her. Anticipation, hope. She would never know why. But she was sure that Hank was near. Some unseen sense warned her. Her heart began to race as she took a deep breath, freezing, waiting

.o0o.

When Hank reached Simmons' office he hesitated. He was so close. Now was not the time to make a mistake. They'd be ready for him. But maybe not as ready as they should be. He'd been pretty quiet downstairs. They might not even know he was in the building.

240

If they were looking at anything they'd be watching the doorknob, waiting for it to twist. It would be their key to shoot.

What about Amy? Where would she be? He had to make sure she didn't get caught in the crossfire. There were more than enough issues to make him hesitate. But he who hesitated, died.

Stepping back, he ran through the door like he was running through a sheet hanging on a clothesline.

The door banged off the back wall as he took in the setting. Amy in a chair. Bennet by the window, Simmons behind his desk.

"Behind the door," Amy yelled.

Without thinking, he spun and emptied a barrel of buckshot hitting Denning in the wrist, leaving just enough to keep it attached. The man screamed as he grabbed his arm and held it to his chest. The pistol fell to the floor with a thud, tangled and twisted.

Hank ignored Denning as he brought the shotgun around in time to see Amy kicking Bennet on the inside of his knee with her heel. The man winced and pulled away while he fought to free his gun from its holster. Hank started to pull the trigger for the second barrel of his shotgun when he realized Amy was too close.

Instead, he stepped forward and swung from the hip, catching Bennet under the chin.

His punch lifted the man off the ground and back into the wall. The man slid down the wall, out like a cat put out for the night.

He was about to follow in to inflict even more damage when Amy yelled, "He's got a gun in his desk drawer."

Hank twisted to see Simmons reaching into the top drawer of his desk, his eyes as big as platters while his fingers searched for his weapon.

This man had to live, Hank thought with regret. Killing him fast would be too easy. At least for now.

Hank leaned forward and shoved the desk back, trapping Simmons against the wall, his arm stuck in the drawer. Hank smiled as he whipped the weapons' butt into the trapped arm resulting in a sharp crack that echoed through the room.

That was an arm that wouldn't be using a gun any time soon.

Now came the fun part. Hank thought as he reached across the desk to grab Simmons by the collar and pull him up and over the desk. He continued to hold him as he brought a fist back and slammed it into the man's nose.

Simmons's eyes glazed over then regained enough focus to try and throw a punch at Hank with his good hand, Hank slipped the punch then twisted Simmons around, grabbed him by the seat of his pants and threw him through the office window.

For years, people would talk about that throw. Charlie was a witness and no one ever called Charlie a liar. Not and lived. No, it was generally acknowledged that not only did Simmons clear the boardwalk overhang. He cleared the horse trough and then the hitching rail beyond that to land in the dusty street with a sickening thud.

Hank glanced at Denning who remained in the corner whimpering over his ruined hand. If he knew the doc, they'd have to cut it off to save the arm. Bennet was still out.

The red rage still boiled inside of him. He needed an enemy. Someone to hurt.

Amy. He twisted to see her looking at him with a strange look. His gut turned over. He'd seen that look before. The look of seeing a monster.

"I knew you'd come," she said as she pulled at the ropes around her wrist.

Hank dropped the shotgun on the desk and pulled his knife to cut her free.

She sighed as the ropes fell away and rubbed at her wrists. She reached for him, but he backed away.

"I'm not done," he said to her. "Jack and Dusty are downstairs, go to them." Then before she could say anything else, he used the shotgun to clear the remaining glass from the window and stepped out onto the overhang to drop down next to Simmons laying in the dirt.

He used his boot to roll the man over and winced. The man had fallen wrong, the arm he hadn't broken had been trapped under him and was laying at an odd angle. Yet the man still breathed.

A crowd had formed, business people, passing cowboys, and miners. Hank ignored them as he continued to study Simmons for a long moment until the man finally opened one eye to stare up at him.

"Be gone by tomorrow," Hank said, "or I won't be so nice the next time. I ever see you again. I'll hang you from the nearest tree. And there ain't anyone man enough to stop me."

Simmons sputtered as if he were going to argue. Hank raised an eyebrow, daring him to complain. But finally, the fallen man stopped and slumped back in on himself, accepting the inevitable.

Hank coughed then spit into the dirt next to the man's head, just to drive home the point.

It was over, he realized with a sense of relief. She was safe. He could once again live in this world. Turning, he found his two friends standing on the boardwalk, Amy between them. Looking at him like he had crawled out from underneath a rock.

Dusty coughed then said, "Seven men, and you didn't kill a one of them."

Hank continued to stare at Amy. "I'm sorry," he said. "There weren't any other way."

She shook her head as she stepped down off the boardwalk and reached for his hand. He pulled back. It was covered in Simmons' blood. She reached again and took his hand in hers.

"Hank Richards," she said as she stared down at his hand. "Don't you ever apologize for saving me."

"You deserve better," he said.

She lifted her head to stare into his eyes. "There is no better."

His insides relaxed. She wasn't walking away from him and the beast inside of him. She was taking him as he was. A man could ask for nothing more. The woman he loved accepting him for who he was.

"It's getting late," he said to her. "We won't make it back to the cabin. Do you want to wait until tomorrow to get married?"

Her brow furrowed as she frowned up at him. "If you think I am waiting to get married you aren't as smart as I thought you were. No, we will be married now and we will spend our wedding night camped next to the river. The stars for a blanket and you to keep me warm."

Hank laughed. God, what a woman.

Epilogue

Amelia stared out the window at San Francisco laid out below them. Hank had insisted on the biggest mansion on Nob Hill. She bounced little Rebecca on her hip while her son, Jack, played with his toys on the oriental rug in her husband's library. The boy loved building complex towers out of blocks then knocking them down.

Hank would come here first, she knew. After six years, she had grown to know her husband's habits well.

As she looked down at the distant bay she marveled once again at how lucky she was. Yet, there was something she needed to discuss with her husband. Something sensitive and as she well knew. Hank didn't do sensitive very well.

She heard the front door open and Jenkins greet Hank. She knew that her husband would hand the butler his hat and coat. Yes, there were his steps on the polished hardwood floor. She would know that sound anywhere. Her heart jumped. Even after all these years, she still became excited.

The door opened and her big strong husband stepped in. He was as handsome as ever. A fine suit of clothes, polished shoes. So different than the man she had first seen in Charlie's shack back in Reno.

"Papa," Little Jack yelled as he raced across the room to throw himself at his father. Hank lifted him up, into a tight hug. Then placed him back on the ground. That was so their relationship she thought. No need for too much emotion. Just enough to cement their closeness then back to being normal.

"How'd it go?" she asked him.

He shrugged his wide shoulders. "Pretty much like I expected. We are richer this quarter than we were last. And we'll be richer the next."

He bent down to give the baby a quick kiss and tickle her chin. The little girl giggled and looked up at her father like he was her hero. Then he leaned over and kissed his wife. Her insides melted just like they always did when they kissed. But before she could follow it up with a second kiss, he pulled back and stared out the window.

She saw it on his face, that lost look of unhappiness. This was what she wanted to talk to him about. But if she approached it wrong, he'd crawl into his cave and never deal with the issue bothering him.

"What else did they say?" she asked him.

He sighed heavily without pulling his gaze from the window. "They're opening the shaft across the valley on that far ridge. You know where I took out that other claim. The engineers think it will pay pretty good," he scoffed.

She smiled to herself. Her husband knew more about mining than any of the men they had hired. She also knew that he missed that life.

"We have a problem," she told him.

He immediately turned away from the window to look at her with a concerned expression.

"Neither of us like living here." There, the words were out.

He frowned at her. She placed a hand on his chest. "Hank, you know it is true. I can feel you being pulled away. I find you staring off into the distance ..."

"That doesn't mean I don't want to be here."

She scoffed. "Last week, you were out digging in the back yard. I swear if our gardener, Pascal, hadn't stopped you. You would have dug halfway to China."

"Amy ..."

"No, Hank. This isn't for us. I miss Rebecca and Jenny. I miss cooking you dinner instead of some woman I barely know."

He continued to frown at her, but behind his eyes, there was something new. Perhaps a hope.

"I don't want our children growing up like this," she continued. "I spent the morning trying to think of some chore for Jack to do. Something he could be responsible for. I couldn't come up with anything that wouldn't make a servant upset."

"Amy ..."

"No, I'm serious," she said. "I'm not saying we need to live in a log cabin in the backwoods. Although, there are times it sounds magical. No, but a nice ranch in the foothills of the Eastern High Sierra. Some place where you can build and work. Sitting behind a desk is killing you slowly."

His brow softened as he sighed heavily then he laughed. "I've been trying to figure out a way to bring it up. But I thought you'd be upset. We'd gotten to the top. I thought you'd never want to walk away."

She laughed as she laid her head on his chest so he could put his arm around her. "Hank Richards. All I ever wanted was to be your wife and that means letting you be the man you need to be."

He sighed heavily then leaned down and kissed the top of her head. "God, do you ever think what our lives would have been like if I hadn't been walking by that alley at that exact moment."

She shuddered then leaned back to look up into his eyes. "You would have found me. We were meant to be together."

He laughed. "You just remember that next winter when you're stoking a stove and cursing the thought of cooking me breakfast."

She laughed with him as her heart filled with happiness. This was her man and he loved her. A woman could ask for nothing more.

The End

Author's Notes

Thank you for reading 'Sweetwater Ridge,' the third book in the 'High Sierra' series.

I would love to know what you think of it. My readers make it possible for me to do what I love, so I am always grateful and excited to hear from you. Please stop by my website GLSnodgrass.com or send me an Email at GL@GLSnodgrass.com. Feel free to sign up for my newsletter. I use my newsletter to announce new releases and give away free books. Or you can follow me on **Amazon Author Page** Or via Bookbub at **https://www.bookbub.com/authors/g-l-snodgrass.** I also post on my Facebook page. **https://www.facebook.com/G.L.Snodgrass/ f**

As always, I would like to thank my friends for their assistance with this book. Sheryl Turner, Anya Monroe, Eryn Carpenter, and Kim Loraine. I couldn't have done it without them.

If you enjoyed 'High Desert Cowboy' please tell a friend or two. And please help out by rating this book at Amazon, Bookbub, or Goodreads. Reviews from readers make a huge difference for a writer.

I have added the first two chapters of one of my Regency novels that I think you might like. 'The American Duke'

Again,   thank   you.

The American Duke

Chapter One

Sometimes life turns out better than a girl could ever hope. That night was such a night for Miss Lydia Stafford.

That very morning, she had been introduced to the Queen. Her, a simple country girl. And tonight. This ball. All in her honor. It was almost too much to believe. Smiling to herself, she sighed heavily. She had danced with a Duke, two Earls, and a very handsome young Baron. And each of them had looked at her as if she were a woman. Not a silly school girl.

A delicious feeling of power and satisfaction washed through her. What girl wouldn't love this life? Especially when compared to a country cottage with a leaky roof.

For the thousandth time, she sent up a silent prayer of thanks. All of this was because her sister had married a Duke. It was His Grace, the Duke of Norwich who was paying for this fairytale. It was only because of him and his status that these people accepted her.

She was perfectly aware, if not for Ann's marriage, her best hope of matrimony would have been a tradesman or farmer. Instead, she had been admitted to the inner sanctum of British nobility.

Running her gloved hands over her silk blue dress she couldn't help but smile. Both Ann and the Duke's Mother, the Dowager Duchess of Norwich had insisted she wear a high waisted, pastel. Lydia had refused. Repeatedly, until they had finally relented.

Instead, she wore dark blue with a true waist. Silk, not cotton. A look she instinctively knew that men preferred.

Ann and the Dowager just wanted her to be accepted by the other women of the ton. But Lydia looked at it differently. She wanted to be noticed by the men of the ton.

The other young women coming out this year could afford to be nondescript. They drew power from fitting it. From following the rules. From familial connections and a long history of expectations.

Lydia knew that would never be her strength. She hadn't been raised in this world. She had not had a lifetime to make connections. After all, she was a Miss, not a Lady. No, her only hope was to be the diamond in the rough. The one girl who stood out from the crowd. The one who was noticed.

Then, and only then might she capture the attention of someone of worth.

And tonight, the journey began. The simple goal, find a husband before the season ended. And as the Dowager had explained repeatedly. Every choice, every comment, would be weighed and evaluated. Mostly by the mothers of the eligible bachelors.

What The Dowager didn't understand, Lydia thought. She wasn't interested in men who could be swayed by their mother's concerns.

No, her husband would be a prince charming type. Strong, handsome, kind, and adore her. The kind of man who would never let his mother dictate his wife.

Lydia smiled as His Grace, the Duke of Norwich approached her. He bowed slightly while she dropped into a quick curtsy. The two of them lived in the same house and shared every meal. It seemed sort of ridiculous that they follow such formalities. But, it was one of this life's many rules, she realized.

"Standing alone?" he said with a slight shake of his head. "No, aren't you young women supposed to congregate in packs. Like wolves scoping out their target.

Lydia laughed. "Thank you again, Your Grace, for all of this," she said as she waved at the ballroom teaming with people. Nobility, wealth, happiness.

He returned her smile and dipped his head in appreciation.

"You are my sister now," he said. "You and Isobel. Of course you deserve all of this. But be careful."

Her brow furrowed in confusion.

"A beautiful woman," he continued. "Becomes a target. A beautiful woman with a heavy dowry becomes a target for the worst of men."

She studied him for a moment and realized that he really was concerned for her happiness. Once again she thanked her sister for marrying such a fine gentleman. And a very rich one at that.

"Thank you, Your Grace," she said as she lowered her head. "I will keep that in mind."

He sighed heavily as he scanned the crowd then said. "As my sister-in-law, I desperately hope I don't have to take to the dueling fields to protect your honor. But I will. Have no doubt."

The seriousness of his expression and his words drove home the point. She must do nothing that risked her honor or the Duke might very well die in a duel. The thought sent a shaft of self-awareness through her. She was part of a family. Part of a society where the rules were very strict and ruthlessly enforced.

"Of course, Your Grace, I assure you, I will do nothing that brings shame to your … our family."

He smiled gently. "It is not you I worry about Lydia. You I would trust with my soul. No, it is them I worry about," he said as he waved at the partygoers. "They are the most conniving, vindictive, shallow groups of humans on the face of the earth. I am sure of it."

Lydia gasped. How could he say such a thing? This was the British Nobility. The people who ran the country and more and more of the world every day.

Seeing her surprise, he laughed gently. "Don't worry, every other klatch of humans is almost as bad. The only difference is that this group has all the power. And at times, it can go to their head."

Lydia frowned as she tried to process his words. Why had she never heard him speak like this before? Why now?

Obviously seeing her confusion, he smiled and said, "You are an adult now. It is time you knew the truth. The world is filled with carnivores. Do not allow yourself to become their prey."

"Does Ann know you think this way?" Lydia asked.

The Duke smiled, "She's the one who told me to talk to you." The twinkle in his eye let her know just how true that was. "She believed," he continued. "You might listen to me whereas, in her words, 'if she told you the sky was blue, you would insist it was green.'"

Lydia's cheeks grew warm. She and her sister had been known to disagree on a thing or two of late. They were close, just as she and Isobel were close. But that didn't mean they always got along. They were sisters after all.

Still, the thought that Ann didn't think she knew how to be careful was idiotic. It wasn't like she had been raised in a glass jar. She and her two sisters had been thrown from their house when she was but eleven. She had lived dirt poor on the kindness of others. No, she knew how harsh life could be.

Smiling back up at the Duke, she said, "My sister should know very well that I have every intention of making a match as perfect as hers. Perhaps even better."

The Duke laughed. "Unfortunately, most of the Dukes are older than dirt and under no circumstances are you to even flirt with one of the Princess. They are blaggards, each one."

Lydia laughed. This was a side of her brother-in-law she rarely saw. Normally, it was the strong, formal Duke persona he presented to the world. But behind that façade was a happy man who liked life.

Ann had done that to him, she realized. Opened him up. Softened the sharp edges and made him a better man. And a perfect brother-in-law.

"I assure you," she said. "No blaggards, as you called them. No beasts, as Isobel refers to them. No, I will marry a kind, gentle man."

He smiled. "With a title, I assume?"

She blushed slightly. "Well, after all, I am a woman and status is important. But the right man is more important, don't you think?"

He pursed his lips as he thought about it then shrugged. "You know your own mind."

Lydia sighed internally. Yes, she did. As almost every girl, she had dreamt of her future husband most of her life and was determined to accept nothing less than exactly what she wanted in a partner for life.

As they stood next to each other watching the dancers twist and turn in the quadrille she could only smile to herself. So refined, so … as things should be. Yes, her life was special.

As the music came to a halt. She watched as her sister bowed to her partner, the Earl of Brookenham. His Grace's good friend. The two of them laughed about something and turned to make their way towards them.

The Earl of Brookenham? She thought. What of him? He would make an excellent husband. As half the women of the ton were perfectly aware. They talked of little else. Rich, a long and illustrious family. Handsome, tall. With a kind smile and an easy laugh.

Yet, deep in her soul, she knew it was not right.

There was no spark between them. Nothing but casual friendship. No butterflies. No anxiety. And from everything she had ever heard. Butterflies were mandatory for falling in love. And the one thing she was sure of was that she would never marry a man she didn't love.

Besides, her sister Isobel hated the man for some unknown reason. Despite their age difference. Put the two of them in the same room and it was like two of Isobel's barn cats meeting on a trail. Neither would back down.

No, the Earl of Brookenham was not a candidate. But the thought did not distress her. She had an entire year and a plethora of eligible men to choose from. It was only a matter of finding him.

"So," her sister said to her before she turned and smiled up at her husband. "Are you enjoying yourself, Lydia?"

Lydia smiled as she nodded. "Yes, everything is so perfect."

Lord Brookenham laughed gently. "And to make it even better for you. Your sister Isobel is upstairs, furious that she cannot participate."

Lydia laughed. "You know me too well, My Lord."

Her brother-in-law laughed as he shook his head, "Yes, Well, next year when Isobel comes out, I fear the ton will not know what hit them."

Both Lydia and Ann smiled to each other. Their younger sister was known to be rather forceful. Some would even say blunt, in expressing her opinions.

Lord Brookenham scoffed as he scowled. "I plan to spend the season on my estates. It will be the only safe place in Britain I fear."

"What, you worry about a young girl?" His Grace said to his good friend with a teasing smirk.

Lord Brookenham scoffed again. "I have a mother who is perfectly capable of pointing out my many failings. I don't need a sixteen-year-old girl for that."

The group laughed, That was Isobel without a doubt.

"There you are," The Duke's mother, the Dowager of Norwich said as she approached them, completing the group. "You should be dancing, my dear," she added, addressing Lydia

Lydia smiled at the older woman as she dropped a quick curtsey. "Yes, Your Grace, But the next dance is to be a waltz and I have been informed by more than one senior female member of the ton, that I am not to dance the waltz."

The Dowager nodded, "All the more reasons for you to dance all the other dances, my dear. You don't want people thinking the wrong thing. That you are unwanted as a dance partner. That is how stories spread."

Lydia glanced over at her brother-in-law. Was this what he meant by the ton being conniving and vindictive.

He raised an eyebrow and smiled just the slightest bit, letting her know that was exactly what he had meant.

Then he turned to his wife and held out his hand as he said, "A waltz? Then I believe I have this dance."

His wife looked up at him with adoring eyes and blushed slightly. Lydia couldn't help but smile. It was one of their silly rules, Ann was only allowed to dance the waltz with her husband. The rest of the ladies of the ton thought it was unbecoming. And rather possessive. After all, there were many women who would love to dance the waltz with a handsome Duke. But unfortunately, because he was a Duke, they could not complain directly to him, heightening their frustration.

What they didn't understand was that Ann loved the fact that her husband was jealous enough to demand that she dance the waltz with him alone. Besides, although, Ann was everything sweet and kind, she rather enjoyed upsetting the other women of the ton. Especially when it came to her husband.

Lydia could only smile as she watched the two of them walk out onto the dance floor.

"Brookenham," the Dowager said to him with a frown as she snapped her fan open and began to wave it. "Isn't their someone you need to dance with. Go, go make some woman's night by asking her to dance. There aren't enough eligible bachelors here tonight for you to be wasting your time here to the side."

Lord Brookenham grimaced as he bowed to The Dowager. Lydia could see behind his eyes that the man couldn't wait to get away. He nodded to her then hurried away.

Once he was gone, the Dowager turned to her and slowly shook her head. "Really Lydia, spending all your time here alone. You must mix, you must mingle. How else are you to impress some mother who will insist you meet her son? Even worse, you will never learn the latest gossip unless you let them impress you with their knowledge. It is all part of the game."

Lydia could only frown. She had no real friends in this world other than her sisters. The Dowager had made every effort over this last year to expose her to more and more of the senior members of the ton and their daughters. But there had been no connection. Not really.

The other girls didn't look at life the way she did. They had grown up pampered, always knowing they would live at the highest levels of society. The rules and expectations had been drilled into them from an early age.

Besides, she knew in her very soul that they looked down on her. A simple country Miss. Not even from London. Growing up in the wilds of Kent or some such foreign place. Of

Of course, they had been perfectly accepting. Much like a snake accepts its prey. But Lydia knew the truth behind those sweet smiles and cold eyes. She was a threat. Competition on the marriage market.

She knew she would never truly fit in. Never be accepted as truly one of them. On the other hand, she had never expected to live her dream.

She was more than willing to accept the trade-off.

"Why is gossip so important, Your Grace?" Lydia asked. "Besides, I was always taught that gossip was frowned upon. Unladylike."

The Dowager harrumphed as she continued to fan herself.

"Gossip is the coin of the realm, my dear. Never forget that. You have to know what is happening within the ton to ensure you do not take a fatal step."

Lydia frowned at the Dowager as she tried to understand.

The older woman rolled her eyes and said, "Imagine if you were to hear a rumor that Lady Gleason is increasing. A fact that everyone knows. And you were to congratulated Lord Gleason the next time you danced with him.

Lydia nodded as she waited for a more detailed explanation. Although she had no idea who Lady Gleason was or why she would ever dance with Lord Gleason.

"It might," the Dowager continued, "be important to know that Lady Gleason and Lord Gleason hate each other and have not been in the same room with each other for over two years. Do you think that little tidbit of information might be important? That, plus the fact that the child might very well be that of her footman. Or at least that is the rumor."

Lydia swallowed heavily as she nodded. A cold feeling trickled down her spine as she imagined asking the man to his face. Or worse, in front of his wife. The Lady might very well think she had done it to bring shame to her. She might very well have created an enemy for no good reason.

"Or," the Dowager said. "The latest about the Marquis of Treadbury and his brother Lord Drake."

Lydia frowned, "Who are they and why should I care?"

The Dowager shook her head obviously upset that Lydia didn't know what she should. "The heirs to the Duke of Cambridge?"

"What about them?"

"They are dead," the Dowager said with an angry scowl. "A carriage accident in Oxford."

Lydia winced, but still, she didn't seem to understand the significance.

"It means," she said with an exasperated tone. "That there are two fewer eligible bachelors. What is more, while there was a third son to inherit, no one has seen him in ten years or so. A young man named Aaron. Supposedly, he ran off to the wilds of America. And if they don't find him alive and soon, then the title will revert to the crown."

Lydia pondered the idea of a young man abandoning all that wealth and power. What must have driven him away? But he had also abandoned his responsibility. Again, why?

"And just so we are perfectly aware," the Dowager continued. "We, the ton, cannot abide the ideas of titles returning to the crown. Too few of us and we lose our power."

Lydia nodded, it sort of made sense. But still, what kind of man would abandon his family and his country?

A scoundrel without a doubt, she thought as she remembered what His Grace had told her about blaggards. Most assuredly, a man who met every criteria for the word.

Chapter Two

The air tasted of pine with a hint of cedar. A faint breeze brought the distant call of an eagle while the river rumbled along like it had since the mountains rose from their grave.

Aaron Drake sighed with contentment as he dipped his oar and steered the birch bark canoe around a huge rock sitting in the middle of the river. Glancing over his shoulder he watched as his friend, *Be'-ah-ish*, Gray Wolf, made the same maneuver.

Focusing forward, Aaron could only marvel once again at the majesty of this land. A beautiful but hard country, he reminded himself. Ten years and it never stopped to amaze him. The majestic mountains, the dense forests, the way life was lived on the edge. The wrong move, the wrong decision easily led to disaster. Yet it was filled with bounty.

As was rather obvious by the bundles of beaver pelts filling his canoe. Two more days and they would make the York Factory, the Hudson Bay Company's main trading post. There they would trade their pelts for supplies and return to Gray Wolf's people on the Snake river half-way across the continent.

Aaron smiled to himself. There had been no need to come this far. They had passed several trading posts on their trip but Gray Wolf wanted to see the world of *Tavyoh*, the white man's world.

So, the York Factory it was. Besides, Aaron wouldn't mind a few weeks with his own. Catching up on the world and all of its troubles. Then it would be once more into the wilds. A free trapper in search of fur.

He smiled to himself, they hadn't even gotten there yet and he was already looking forward to getting away. Would this wanderlust ever leave him, he wondered. Would he ever tire of crossing the next mountain just to see what was on the other side?

"Probably not," he mumbled to himself. Accepting the reality of who he was. A man who loved adventure.

The two of them continued downriver. Silent, passing through without leaving a mark.

"*Wai'yapoo*," Gray Wolf hissed, Nighthawk, the name he had been given by Gray Wolf's band over four years earlier.

Looking up, Aaron saw his friend pointing to the far shore, further down the river.

A cold shiver ran down Aaron's spine. A large male grizzly stood on the bank sniffing the wind. Rearing up on his hind legs. Over ten feet. The monster was huge and scarred from a life of fighting and killing.

It dropped back down to all four feet on the ground and stared at them. There was no fear in those eyes. Aaron saw. This animal feared nothing in this world. It knew only prey and enemies. Things that must be destroyed or devoured.

Aaron rolled his shoulder as it reminded of his run-in with a black bear six years earlier. The wound still ached on cold mornings. The same bear that in addition to opening his shoulder had left a scar deep in his memory.

It had been but a black bear, not long from its mother's care. This beast, however, here on the banks of the Hayes River was three times larger. There would be no escaping if he ever got a hold of a man.

The memory of that black bear made him shiver inside. It was only luck that the bear had exposed its neck to his knife. As a result. he'd traded that bear's pelt for a horse at Fort Vancouver. Then lost that very horse to a broken leg up in the Yellowstone country the next spring. The thought sent an anger through him. He'd liked that horse.

Capturing his friend's attention, Aaron nodded. They were perfectly safe, there in the middle of the river, but Aaron also made plans to ensure they camped on the opposite bank. The last thing he wanted was this beast's hot breath waking him in the middle of the night just before it clamped down on his skull.

No, he had learned early. In this country, it never paid to tempt fate. There were too many ways to die. And almost all of them painful. God how he loved it so.

Two days later, Gray Wolf and he pulled their canoes up onto the beach outside the fort known as York Factory. His friend remained silent as he studied his new surroundings. Aaron joined him for a moment to orient himself.

The Cree villagers outside the fort seemed to have increased. Or maybe it was just the time of year, but without a doubt, there must have been at least a thousand judging by the number of tepees.

Turning, Gray Wolf pointed to a ship moored at the wharf further down the beach. "A mighty *siakki*?" he said in his broken English using the Shoshoni word for canoe. The two of them had spent their time together teaching each other their languages until they had fallen into a habit of mixing and matching.

"Ship," Aaron answered as he began to pull his pelt bales from his canoe and place them above the high tide line.

Gray Wolf nodded as he looked out over the vast Hudson Bay. Aaron studied him for a moment and wondered what he was thinking. But of course, he would never know and he would never presume to ask.

The two of them had an unspoken agreement. They talked of things and told stories, the more outrageous the better. But deep inner thoughts, never. That left a man too exposed.

"Come, we must hurry, I want a whiskey, a bath, and a woman. In that order."

Gray Wolf nodded as he picked up two bundles and easily carried them towards the fort. Aaron could only shake his head. Aaron towered over him, at several inches over six feet he towered over most men. But with a barrel chest and arms like iron ropes, the Indian was stronger than almost any man he'd ever met.

Once they entered the fort, Gray Wolf balked as his nose registered the strange smell. A strong combination of cooked meat, hides being tanned, and too many people. But different than the smell of an Indian village. Some other scent that reminded Aaron of the world he had left at sixteen half a world away.

Aaron pushed past his friend. He would have to adjust. There wasn't much he could do about the stink.

Gray Wolf's brow narrowed as he fell into line behind Aaron.

The door of the main trade building slammed open as two men fell out and onto the ground wrestling. Both men were dressed in buckskin, obviously trappers like himself. Punching and pulling as they rolled across the ground.

The bigger of the two quickly pinned the smaller man then reached back to grab a knife from his belt.

Aaron swallowed hard as he reached down to stop the man from slicing his opponent from stem to stern.

"That's enough," Aaron said as his hand grabbed onto the fighter's wrist like an iron clamp. The man pulled, but Aaron refused to budge, instead, holding that arm in mid killing stroke.

He stared down into the fighter's eyes and shook his head. The man looked up and growled, obviously upset at being denied the chance to kill his enemy. Gray Wolf stood to the side, the butt of his long musket resting in the dirt, his arms folded, as he watched these strange men.

Aaron continued to stare at the man until at last the trapper cursed then leaned to the side to allow his enemy to escape.

"You need to be careful who you interfere with, my friend." the man said as he twisted his arm away. "That's a good way to end up with a knife in your ribs,"

Now that the smaller man had escaped and was running across the square, Aaron let the wrist go.

The man huffed as he stood up. Almost as tall as Aaron, the man was big around the belly and smelled like a dead skunk on a hot day. The man scowled at him, obviously very angry at being denied. It was an unspoken rule amongst the trappers that men did not interfere in another's fight.

"What's your name? my friend," the man spat, obviously not meaning the last part of his question.

Aaron shrugged, "Drake, Aaron Drake. And you?"

The man froze as color slowly drained from his face. Obviously, he had heard of the name and knew of his reputation. Even in this vast land, men told stories about each other and word spread. Who to avoid, who to admire. Who would cheat you out of your back teeth and who could be trusted in a fight.

Aaron cocked an eyebrow, waiting for an answer.

The man swallowed then looked over at Gray Wolf standing there, impassive, rock steady. "I heard about you," the man said with an angry scowl mixed with a tinge of worry. "You're the one that killed Carter at Fort Williams Din't you?"

"It was a fair fight," Aaron growled.

The man studied him for a moment, "And there was that time against the Hidatsa, you were the only bastard to make it out alive."

Aaron nodded as he bit down on his back teeth. Some of those memories he would have preferred to keep good and buried.

Instead, he simply nodded to the man, picked up his bales of fur, and stepped into the trade building.

The clerk looked up, obviously surprised to see them. Aaron was one of the few free traders. Refusing to work directly for the company. Few of the free traders came this far east. It was cheaper and easier to trade at the inland posts.

"Did I hear you say you're Aaron Drake?" the clerk asked with a deep frown.

Aaron nodded.

"Got something for you," the man said as he turned to go into a back room. "Came a couple of months ago," he called out. "Here it is. Was going to send it up to Fort Williams with the next supply train. Someone said they saw you there a few years ago."

Aaron's stomach clenched into a tight ball as he tried to figure out why anyone would be sending him something.

The clerk stepped out of the room with an aged envelope.

"It's got one of those family crest things," the man said as he handed it over. "Why you know people like that?"

Aaron ignored him as he fought to control the nervous energy building inside of him. Turning the letter over, he examined the red-wax seal and sighed internally. It was as he feared.

Pulling the knife from his belt, he used it to slice the letter open. He took a deep breath as he unfolded it and began to read.

Son

I must inform you that your brothers are dead. You are to return to take up their duties. You are to make haste for I fear I am not long for this world myself. I know that we parted with bitter words. But those must be put aside. Your family needs you.

Cambridge

Aaron re-read the letter. The script was jagged as if the old man's hand had shaken while he wrote it. At least the bastard had written it himself and not had one of his lawyers do it. That was something.

Sighing, he let his hands drop as he turned to look back out the front door. His two brothers. Gone. A sadness washed through him.

"I have to return to my father's land," he said to Gray Wolf. "My family needs me and it is something that only I can do."

His friend simply raised an eyebrow as he nodded. He well-understood family obligations. Family, band, tribe, those were all that mattered in his world. "You have told me that your father is a chief in your world?"

Aaron nodded. "And I am to take up his duties."

Again, Gray Wolf nodded. "Then I go with you. To this En-ga-land, you speak of."

Aaron turned back to his friend. "It is very far, a cold wet place."

Gray Wolf almost smiled. "Colder than a bad winter in the Duck Valley?"

Aaron shivered, no, not that cold, nothing was that cold. "It will be strange. My people will not be as accepting of you as yours were of me."

The Indian nodded, That was not unusual at all. The Blackfeet, the Sioux, many tribes would not have accepted him. "Will I be let to leave to return to my people after going to this En-ga-land?"

Aaron nodded.

Gray Wolf grunted then said, "I will return with stories. Memories for my old years. What more can a man hope for?"

Aaron sighed internally as a small jealousy filled him. His friend was free to return to this land. Free to do as he wished. He, however, had just lost such freedom.

Looking down at the letter in his hand, he slowly shook his head and mumbled under his breath, "Damn you father."

'The   American   Duke'

Sweetwater Ridge

CPSIA information can be obtained
at www.ICGtesting.com
Printed in the USA
LVHW041128111119
636959LV00006B/2029